Smith's
MONTHLY

Every Month Original Novels, Stories, and Articles

USA Today Bestselling Writer
Dean Wesley Smith

TABLE OF CONTENTS

SHORT STORIES

FULL NOVEL

NONFICTION

Smith's Monthly Issue #41

Introduction
A CHARACTER'S NAME

Writers are a strange bunch and I fit right into that strangeness.

(And right now all my friends are nodding.)

Writers pick at things, at life, at details, always feeding that little writer voice in our heads.

It would be impossible to count how many times I have watched the same show or movie or read the same book to try to figure out how something was done by another writer. All long-term writers have a hunger to learn how to tell better stories.

Long-term professional writers also ask accountants and lawyers some of the strangest questions. In our business, our property can be controlled by our estate for seventy years past our deaths. That brings up some very, very strange questions.

In public we may look normal, but writers will sit in airports or waiting rooms and make up entire life stories of the people around them, without ever asking a question of anyone.

I have created more serial killers sitting in airports than I care to think about.

But writers, as a group, tend to really get nuts about names.

We love names.

A lot of writers haunt graveyards, not because the writer writes horror, but because of the names on the gravestones. And yes, I have done that more than once or twice. A bunch more.

And writers I know sit through credits of movies, not just to see the Marvel gag at the end, but with a notebook and pen to get ideas for names of characters.

I can't begin to tell you how many times a waitress or waiter has come up to me and I see their name tag and they have a cool name and I flat out ask them where the name came from.

Names do so much for writers and our creative voices.

For example, Lee Child tells a story about how, before he started writing novels, his wife would ask him to get stuff off of top shelves. (He's very tall.) And people in grocery stores would ask him as well. So he started to be known as the "reacher." He thought it a cool name and thus was born Jack Reacher, the main character that made him very rich.

The entire novel in this issue came from a character name.

Tombstone Canyon is one of the books in my Thunder Mountain series, and it started when one day I was reading a book on the history of Idaho mining and I saw the name Tombstone.

No first or last, just Tombstone.

I liked that and added the name Dan to it.

So I had a character.

And with the name Tombstone Dan, I knew he had to be in my Thunder Mountain series.

And I had to tell the story of how he got the name in 1902.

That's enough for me as a writer. I sat down and off I went, telling the story of Tombstone Dan.

I sure hope you enjoy it as much as I enjoyed writing it. I had fantastic fun bringing Tombstone Dan to life.

And thanks for the support of this crazy magazine project. It means a lot to me.

—Dean Wesley Smith
July 15th, 2017

Now Available!

Five-Story Collections in Some of Dean Wesley Smith's Most Popular Series. Find them at your favorite booksellers!

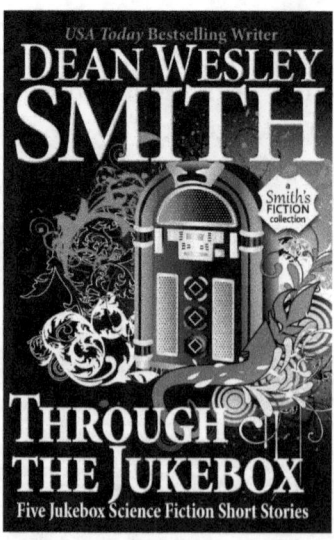

Coming Next Issue in *Smith's Monthly*

DEATH TAKES A DIAMOND

A Mary Jo Assassin Novel

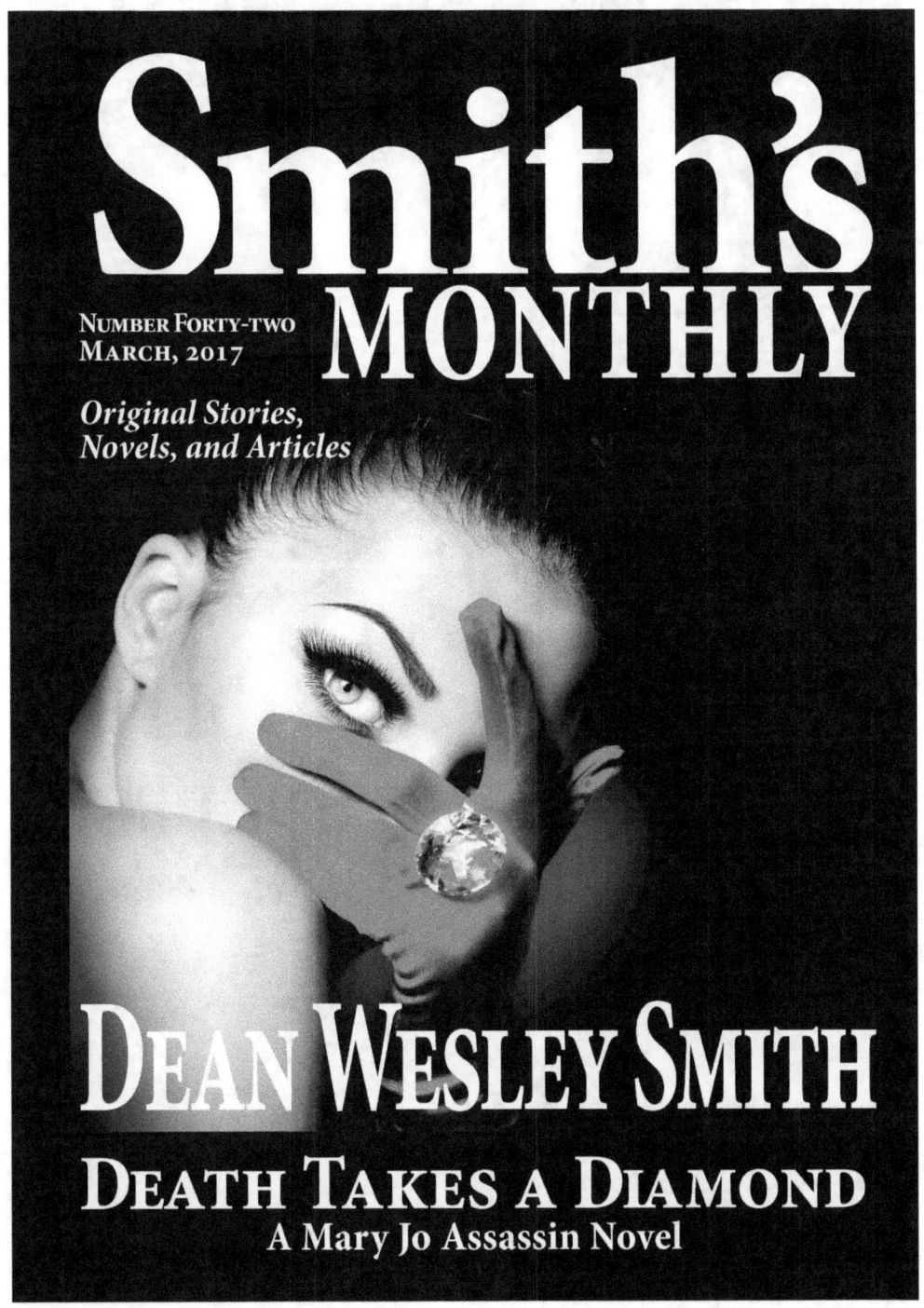

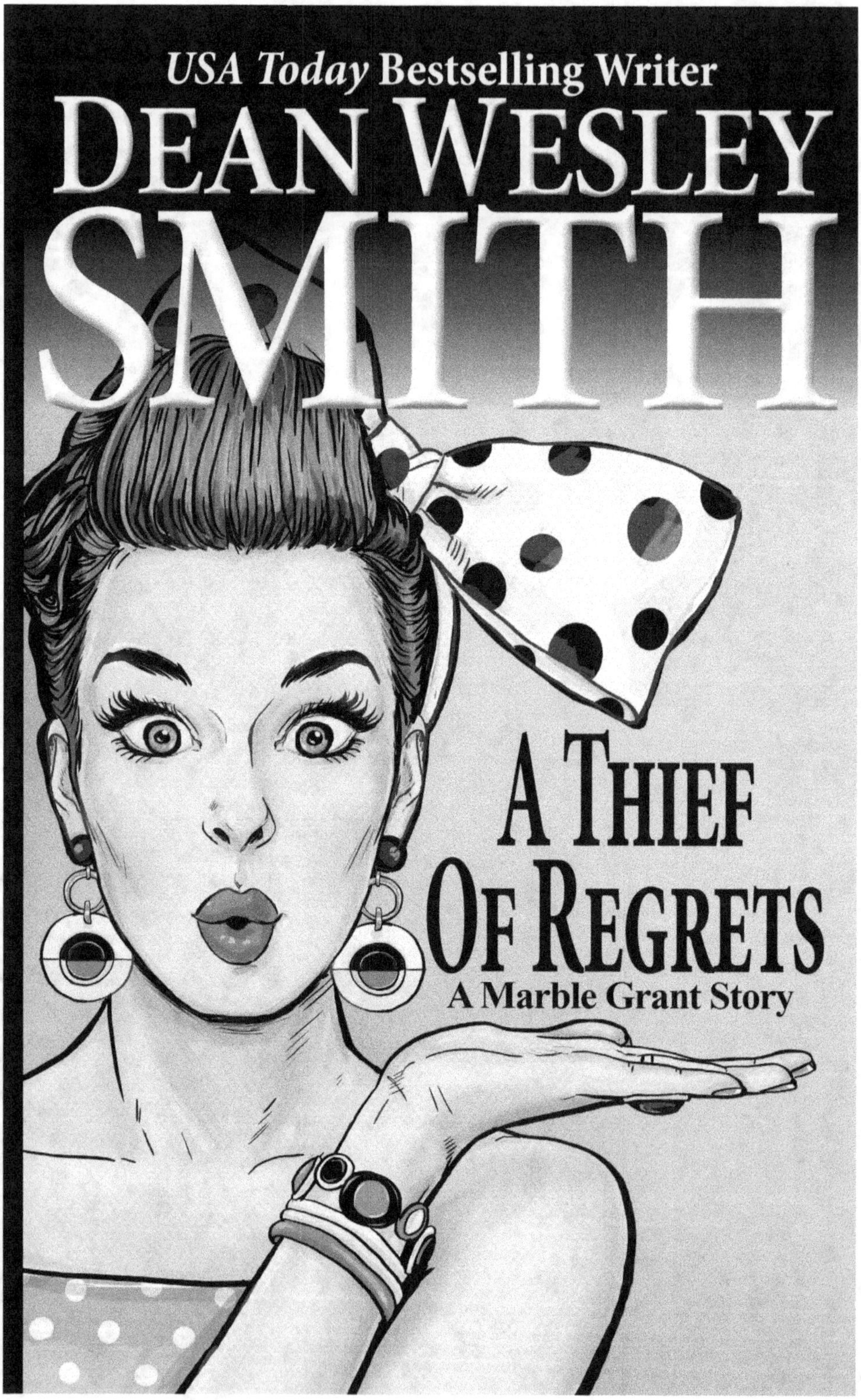
USA Today Bestselling Writer
DEAN WESLEY
SMITH
A THIEF
OF REGRETS
A Marble Grant Story

Marble Grant's partner and lover Sim discovered her old boyfriend still pined after her, even though Sim died months earlier.

The poor guy needed help. And who better to give him that help but two ghosts?

With a little assist from Poker Boy and Patty Ledgerwood, they might help him survive.

The fourth story in the growing Marble Grant saga.

A THIEF OF REGRETS
A Marble Grant Story

ONE

I HAD COME to love being dead.

Yeah, sounds like the bullet in my forehead actually had scrambled my ghost brains as well as my live ones. Or I had simply gone batty.

I suppose both were a possibility. But I hadn't questioned why I liked being dead until today.

Today started like any other wonderful day since I had died.

I crawled out of Sim's and my massive soft bed right at the crack of noon, went into the kitchen as naked as the day I was born, which was over a hundred years ago, and got a cup of coffee before heading back to the shower.

Since I was dead, very few people could see me, but I wouldn't have cared. Even dead I didn't look a day over twenty-eight and had never been the shy type.

And since I was dead, I sure didn't plan on aging, so the only thing that would change would be my hair color, something Sim said I changed as fast as the weather.

Of course, we lived in a wonderful condo in Vegas, where the weather didn't change that often, so my gut sense is that my hair was ahead of the weather by a factor of two.

Today it was a light blue.

A dead girl has to have a hobby after all.

I was done with my shower and sipping a second cup of coffee and eating a wonderful bagel with cream cheese on our deck when my love showed up and joined me.

Sim kissed me and sat down with a sigh.

The air was getting warm and it felt wonderful against my skin. I had dressed in my normal comfortable jeans, silk blouse, and tennis shoes.

Sim was dressed about the same. And since we were almost exactly the same height and body type, our closets were joint closets. Worked out great that way.

But now this early afternoon I felt great and she was frowning.

She was a morning person and got out to help people while I slept. Then we both worked afternoons together, spent the evenings relaxing together, then I went out and worked evenings on my own while she went off to bed.

So the frown told me she must have had a rough session with someone this morning and the memory wasn't fading fast enough.

As Ghost Agents, our main job is to spot people who need help and then, by getting inside their heads, figure out what we can do for them.

What lived in a lot of people's minds could really shock a person. I was still getting shocked almost every day.

The Ghost Agents who trained us, Jewel and Tommy, said they still were shocked sometimes at the ugliness in some people, or the incredible beauty in others.

"Want to talk about it?" I asked, sipping my black coffee and enjoying the view of the Strip.

Sim just shrugged. "Ran into an old friend is all."

"From Boise?" I asked, now turning to face her completely.

Neither of us had talked much about our lives before becoming ghosts. To be honest, it just had never occurred to me.

We had both been friends with Patty Ledgerwood, although we had never met each other. Patty was also a superhero like we are, or were before we became Ghost Agents. We are still working to regain some of our superhero powers.

Patty and her boyfriend, Poker Boy, bought us this condo and all the stuff in it for us to live in.

Sim nodded to my Boise question. "Guy by the name of Stanton, also in banking. He and I had a fling about three months before I died. A really nice guy. Very smart and very sweet."

"Was he good in bed?" I asked, smiling at her and trying to lighten the mood a little.

Sim smiled, clearly in the memory. "Let's just say he did what he needed to do."

"Oh, I like the sounds of that."

She laughed and gave me that seductive wink. "If you're a good girl, I'll tell you every detail later."

"I'm wearing a halo for the rest of the day," I said.

Again she laughed.

"So seeing him got you down?" I asked. "Or did he have something going on with him otherwise?"

Her smile vanished and she nodded. "Not sure what to do."

"Play out what happened for me," I said, reaching across the table and holding her hand. Even in the heat her skin felt cool.

"I saw him down in the MGM Grand lobby early this morning," Sim said. "I almost didn't recognize him. He looked tired, run-down, and clearly depressed. All the signs that Jewel and Tommy taught us to watch for in people who needed help."

I nodded and let her go on.

"So I went to him and inside his head to see what was the problem."

She sat there in silence, the only sounds around us were from the city traffic six flights below.

"And what was the problem?" I asked after a minute."

"My death was the problem," she said.

That set me back.

"It seems," she said, "he was in love with me. Or thought he was. He was very confused. I thought it was just a fling, but after I died it seemed to mean more. He felt like he had lost the love of his life and has been going downhill ever since. But he didn't feel that way before I died."

"Oh, shit," I said softly.

Sim nodded. "He lost his job last week and decided to come to Las Vegas to see if he could get more information from Patty about me and my death, if he could find her. So far he hasn't."

"Oh, shit," I said once again.

If there was ever an "oh shit" moment, this was it.

Sim looked up at me, those wonderful blue eyes drilling right into me as she could do.

"Have you given one thought to the people we knew when we were alive?"

Again that question shocked me.

I hadn't.

Not one thought, not even enough to go see who was at my memorial service, if anyone gave one.

It flat hadn't occurred to me.

Damn it all to hell. Why hadn't I?

"No," I said, staring back into the eyes of the woman I loved. "And that doesn't seem right and doesn't seem like me at all."

"It's not like me either," Sim said. "And I haven't either until this morning. We should have been helping the people like Stanton move on with their lives, not just ignore them."

"Seems we need some questions answered and then we need to go help some old friends to get past our deaths," I said.

Sim nodded. "Starting with Stanton."

"Answers first," I said, not happy in the slightest that maybe someone had brainwashed us in some fashion or another. I wasn't a fan of being controlled in life, I sure wasn't going to be in death.

Sim just nodded.

TWO

I LOOKED OUT over the city and said simply, "Jewel, we could use your help for a minute."

Jewel appeared and smiled and sat down at the table on the patio with us. She was taller than Sim and I, but dressed almost exactly the same in a silk blouse, jeans, and tennis shoes. She had her hair pulled back and was smiling when she arrived.

"Ever tell you two how much I love this place you have here."

Sim and I both smiled.

"We love it as well," Sim said. "Would you like a bagel or some coffee or water?"

Jewel shook her head. "Just finished lunch. Thanks. So what is the problem?"

"You ever think about the people you left behind when you died?" I asked.

Jewel sat back and shook her head, frowning. "At first, no."

"You did after a time?" Sim asked.

"Tommy and I pushed it after about six months," Jewel said. "We thought we had been brainwashed to not care about our old lives or something."

"I'm feeling that exact same way," I said. "It was as if I didn't even give a thought to the impact of my death on people. And if I was brainwashed, I'm not happy about it."

Jewel nodded. "Both Tommy and I were pretty disgusted at ourselves as well."

"So if not brainwashing, what causes it?" Sim asked.

"Death," Jewel said.

I stared at her for a moment, then at the woman I loved.

Sim looked as confused as I felt.

Jewel glanced up and saw our confusion and smiled. "Here is how it was explained to me and Tommy. If you died and didn't become a Ghost Agent, you'd move into the light and would be able to do nothing for those left behind. Right?"

"But we are Ghost Agents," I said.

Jewel nodded. "But the fact of you dying cleaned out parts of that old life and turned your mind to building a new life."

Sim frowned. "So you mean what happened is a natural part of death?"

"As far as anyone knows," Jewel said. "Yes. Think of it like you have gone from one room to a new room and the door between the rooms closed. Unless you have a specific reason to go back through that door, you don't think about it."

"So there are no rules about us going back and helping people get past our deaths?" I asked.

"None that I have been told," Jewel said. "When Tommy and I came to this same realization, we went back. It wasn't

More Marble Grant Stories
Available at your favorite booksellers.

easy, but we think we helped some of our family and friends a little."

Jewel looked at us. "Did something happen?"

Sim nodded. "Ran into an old boyfriend who has let my death almost destroy him."

"Oh," Jewel said. "Looks like you two have a couple of old lives to clean up a little."

I nodded. "Sure seems that way."

"Call if you need help," Jewel said. "And be braced. The emotions and scars you will find in old family and friends will sometimes be tough to deal with. You don't have to do this, you know."

"Yes, we do," I said. "Now that I know what has happened."

Sim nodded.

With that Jewel vanished.

I reached across and held Sim's hand.

"We have each other to get us through this," I said.

She smiled and squeezed my hand. "We do."

"So let's go see if we can help Stanton," I said.

"Ghosts riding to the rescue," she said.

And we both laughed.

THREE

WE FOUND STANTON right where Sim had left him an hour before. He was leaning against one of the large marble pillars in the massive MGM Grand Hotel lobby, just sort of staring at nothing.

The sound of all the people in the lobby was like a dull roar of a river. And through the large archway across the lobby the sounds of laughter and bells from the casino came echoing in clearly.

There had to be a hundred people in the massive, high-ceilinged lobby.

Stanton looked like he had been handsome, something I would not have been surprised about since Sim had dated him. But Sim was right about how he looked now. Tired and clearly not paying attention to his hair or beard.

He looked depressed and lost.

I also would have seen that from a distance.

"He had heard that Patty works the front desk," Sim said, "and is hoping to recognize her from a description I gave him once."

"Does he feel you might have faked your death and are still alive?" I asked.

"He feels I am still around somewhere, but he doesn't know how or why he feels that way. He even tried a couple counseling sessions and they only made things worse."

"Wow, he might have some borderline superpowers of some sort," I said.

"I was thinking the same thing," Sim said. "His sense about me has clearly driven him, just not in a healthy way."

"And we don't know enough yet to be able to show ourselves to live people," I said.

I knew that was an advanced skill we would pick up given time, but we were both so new, that wasn't going to work. We could barely touch something real at the moment. It felt like we were brushing it.

"Don't know if that would help or make it worse for him," Sim said.

"Somehow we have to convince him he is not going insane," I said, "and just needs to remember you, but let go at the same time."

We had been standing near him having that conversation and for some reason he perked up and started looking around, puzzled, as if he had heard us.

Sim noticed that as well.

"Some superheroes can see us," I said. "I'm starting to think Stanton here is a closet superhero."

Sim nodded. "He's approaching thirty. About the time most superheroes start getting their first powers."

I nodded to that. I stopped aging and got my first powers around twenty-eight and so did Sim.

"We need superhero help," I said.

Sim turned and looked out over the crowd. "Patty, if you can hear me, we need a little help in the MGM Grand lobby."

A voice out of nowhere said, "Be right there."

I laughed. "Who knew we could do that?"

Sim laughed as well. "Nice to know, isn't it?"

Poor Stanton just kept staring around, his head moving back and forth like he was watching a tennis match. One thing for certain, we needed to get him out of here before security came and talked to him about being crazy.

At that moment Patty came walking out from behind the MGM front desk and started toward us.

I jumped Sim and I both to a spot beside her and we fell into step beside her.

"The guy standing beside the pillar is looking for you," Sim said. "He's an old boyfriend who is feeling broken up about my death and that something is wrong. He has come to talk with you."

"He looks like he is in bad shape," Patty said softly without moving her lips.

"He is," Sim said.

"But he could also sense us standing there beside him," I said. "We think he might be a budding superhero."

"We'll find out," Patty said.

Then Patty said, "Need a little help, partner. Out of time in the lobby around

a guy standing near the big pillar I am approaching."

At that moment Stanton saw her walking toward him and smiled.

And with that smile I saw what Sim had seen in him, even for a fling. The guy was hot.

FOUR

"WHAT'S HIS NAME?" Patty whispered to us as we got close.

"Stanton Smith," Sim said.

Patty extended her hand to Stanton. "Mr. Smith, I understand you were looking for me."

"I was," Stanton said, smiling while looking puzzled as he shook her hand. "But I didn't tell anyone that."

At that moment Poker Boy appeared and the entire lobby froze and all the sound vanished.

"Wow," I said, glancing around. "That's cool."

He smiled. "I kind of think it's cool as well. I just slipped us between a moment in time so we could talk."

Patty was using her superpower to calm Stanton, but he still looked like he might bolt at any moment.

"Think we can learn to do this?" I asked.

Poker Boy shrugged. "Not a clue, but would be fun to find out, wouldn't it?"

"It sure would."

"What's happening?" Stanton managed to say.

Patty let go of Stanton's hand she had been holding at that moment and looked at Sim. "You were right, he is a budding superhero."

"A what?" Stanton asked. "And who are you talking to?"

"Sim," Patty said, turning back to face Stanton.

I could feel that she had her full calming power hitting the poor guy. That much would put an elephant to sleep, and it was calming him, but not by much. He was a strong one.

I could sense Poker Boy add his power to her as he touched Patty's arm and Stanton seemed to calm even more. Those two clearly made a wonderful team.

"Think we need Laverne here to figure out which area he's going to work in?" Poker Boy asked.

At that moment Laverne appeared.

Lady Luck herself, standing there in a power suit with her long hair pulled back tight off her face, giving her a stark, business-woman look.

It fit the most powerful woman in the world as far as I was concerned.

She extended her hand to the shocked Stanton. "My name is Laverne. It is a pleasure to meet you."

He shook her hand and nodded. Clearly with even all the calming power of Patty and Poker Boy, he was too stunned to talk.

Can't say as I blame him. Time stops around him and two people just appear in front of him and call him a superhero. If that would have happened to me like it was happening to him, I would have had myself committed as soon as I woke up.

Or I would have sworn off drinking for a month.

"He's going to be working with Adrian in banking and finance," Laverne said to Poker Boy and Patty.

Then she turned to me, then looked directly at Sim. "You two need to help him get past what he has been feeling since you died."

I nodded. So did Sim.

"I'm going to let him be able to see you," Laverne said. "Take him back to your condo and do what you need to to help him get ready to take the next step and get back to work."

Again Sim and I nodded.

"Thank you," Sim said.

At that moment poor Stanton's eyes got wide as suddenly Sim, his dead ex-fling, was standing in front of him.

"Hi, Stanton," Sim said, smiling.

At that, Stanton's eyes sort of rolled up in his head and closed.

I didn't blame him in the slightest. I felt the same way the first time I saw Sim. She was that good-looking.

"Time to move," Poker Boy said.

Poker Boy jumped Stanton and us to our condo, putting the limp Stanton on the couch.

A few minutes later, after Patty could walk back to a dead camera area outside the lobby, she joined us.

"Thanks," Patty said to Poker Boy. "I think we can take it from here."

"Good," he said, kissing his girlfriend on the cheek. "Got a hot ten-twenty no-limit going at the Bellagio."

And he vanished.

Now it was up to the three of us to try to figure out what to do with a very confused, very depressed budding superhero.

I had a hunch we could figure it out.

FIVE

"WE GOING TO** need to get into his head first to see if we can help a little before he wakes up?" I asked.

The three of us had moved to chairs in our living room facing the couch.

The air-conditioning was keeping the condo at a comfortable temperature, even though the day outside had warmed up into the nineties. Our automatic blinds were blocking the sun on one side of the living room, but let in enough light that the room was bright and airy.

"I think we should," Sim said. "But I don't think it should be me in there again. At least not just yet."

"I agree," Patty said.

"So do I," I said.

I stood and moved toward the sleeping man. "Back in a moment. Let me see what I can clean up without changing anything."

I merged inside of Stanton.

Sim was right, since her death he had been majorly conflicted. It seemed what had been a fling to him at the time, when she died, took on more meaning.

I nosed around and discovered that it was his budding superpower that had caused the feeling. He could sense she was still alive, but his rational brain told him otherwise.

And that had set up the conflict.

So I spent about ten minutes just easing his fears, helping him understand a little of what happened, and making him understand that Sim was dead but still around and that he had been right all along.

Just by helping him with those thoughts and blocking some ugly thoughts of hopelessness, I could sense he was feeling better. He had a solid core of good and was clearly a very nice person.

Finally, I suggested he wake up and I left him and went back to my chair.

"He's going to need more work," I said to the worried look on my partner. "But I think in the long run he's going to be fine. He's a really solid and nice guy."

She nodded as Stanton slowly came awake and then looked around. Finally he sat up.

"Was that a dream in the lobby? Am I still dreaming this?"

"Not a dream," Sim said.

Sim pointed to me. "This is my partner and lover, Marble Grant. Marble is another Ghost Agent like I am."

Then Sim indicated Patty. "This is our good friend Patty Ledgerwood. She is a superhero as both Marble and I used to be."

"Superhero?" Stanton asked.

"We'll explain everything," Sim said, smiling. "I promise."

"But you died, didn't you?" Stanton asked.

"I did," Sim said. "Just outside of Vegas in a motorcycle accident."

"And remember the shooting in Boise in the alley about eight months ago where two people were killed?" I asked.

Stanton looked at me. "The real estate agent and her date?"

"That was me," I said, smiling.

He just shook his head and looked at his hands in his lap. "Horrid dream."

I laughed, which surprised him and he looked up.

"Take a look at this view," I said, sweeping my arms in the direction of the city. "Take a look at this fantastic city out there and this amazing condo you are sitting in. Nothing at all horrid about any of it. And you have three people here trying to help you, so that's not so bad either."

"Help me do what?" he asked.

"You came looking for Patty and you found her," Sim said. "You felt there was something more to my death, you sensed it, and you were right, but that conflict tore you apart. Am I right?"

He nodded.

"So now you have found out what happened to me. I am here and working as a Ghost Agent. And because you will soon be getting training as a superhero as well, you can see me."

"I'm no superhero," he said, shaking his head. "I can't even keep a job."

"Because you knew something was different with Sim and the transformation you are going through," I said. "A perfect storm you will soon get under control if you let us help you."

After a moment he did as I thought he would. He nodded.

He was one strong person.

"Good," Patty said, checking her watch. "I got to get to work. Call me or Poker Boy if you need help."

"We'll be fine," Sim said, smiling at Stanton.

Patty nodded and vanished.

"What the hell?" he asked.

"Given some time," I said, smiling at the handsome man sitting on our couch, "you might be able to do that as well."

"She's right," Sim said. "But right now we have a problem."

"What's that?" I asked my wonderful partner.

"He's alive, we're dead. How in the world are we going to get lunch?"

Then it dawned on us both at the same time.

"Take out!"

SIX

OVER THE NEXT few days Stanton got used to living with two women ghosts.

We had a spare bed moved up into our second bedroom and he brought his suitcase from his small hotel to the condo.

After a while the questions he asked were one right after another, some of which we had to call in either Patty or Jewel to help answer.

Having him here actually helped Sim and I learn a lot more about our own place in things. He asked questions we might not have thought of asking for years to come.

I was slowly coming to the conclusion that Stanton was frighteningly smart, much smarter than I had thought when in his head trying to dig through all the confusion.

Twice during the two days he was visited by Adrian, a blonde woman god of finance and banking. Both times they went out onto the patio and talked and both times Stanton came back in smiling. It seemed he really liked his new boss. They clearly talked the same language.

It seemed that as he got to accept the craziness of suddenly being a superhero, he was taking to it quickly. A lot faster than I had done as I slowly grew into my superhero powers.

Of course I didn't have an entire group of people willing to answer questions at the drop of a hat either. I went decades with more questions than answers.

It was on the third day he was there that I forgot about him and staggered out of bed at my normal crack of noon and headed for the kitchen, nude as a baby for my first cup of coffee.

"Now I see why you love her so much," Stanton said from the dining room table.

I glanced over where he and Sim were both smiling at me.

"Yeah," Sim said. "She's hot in a lot of ways."

"No talking in the morning," I mumbled, grabbed my coffee and headed back toward the bedroom.

"Nice ass," Sim said from the dining room.

Stanton just laughed.

And that made me smile. It seemed we had saved one. He said he planned on leaving in a few days to go back to Boise and go back to work.

I was honestly going to miss him. He was such a good guy with a big heart.

But it would be nice to just be back to me and Sim again.

Two days later, the night before he was to leave, Sim rolled over in bed and said softly, "Think Stanton is healthy enough for a three-way with two ghosts?"

I laughed. "Is that even possible?"

She smiled at me that wonderful smile I had come to love in a very short time. "We're learning to touch physical things."

"I'm all the way up to brushing something lightly," I said. Then I laughed. "You know, that might just be enough."

"Exactly what I was thinking," Sim said. "And as we get better at touching things over the years, he could always come back for more tests."

"He's a test subject?" I asked, laughing. "Think he'll mind?"

"From what I saw in his mind," I said, "he's completely heterosexual. I doubt if he's ever had a fantasy about two ghost women, but I know he's thought of two women."

"You up for it?" Sim asked.

"Oh, heavens, yes," I said. "As long as you are with me."

A minute later, as Sim and I crawled into his bed totally naked, Stanton asked if he was dreaming again. He then shuddered and moaned as Sim touched him lightly as an answer.

As I have said over and over since I died, being dead is a ton more fun than being alive.

And for the next two hours with Stanton and Sim, I proved that to myself many times over.

Can't Get Enough of Poker Boy?
These stories and more are
available at your favorite booksellers.

USA *Today* Bestselling Writer

DEAN WESLEY SMITH

A DEAL AT THE END OF TIME

A Seeders Universe Story

Palmer survived the disaster that took most of the human population. He escaped to the mountains to get away from the death.

And there, in a beautiful log home, he started the End of Time Bar, Saloon, and Eatery for any survivor who wanted to drop by.

One Monday morning a very special visitor came by for breakfast.

A Seeders Universe story of survival and fresh starts and good breakfasts.

A DEAL AT THE END OF TIME
A Seeders Universe Story

MONDAY MORNING AT the End of Time Bar, Saloon, and Eatery started off just as every day started. A beautiful sunrise over the mountains to the east painted the sky in reds and pinks and blues that made it impossible to not stop and stare.

And Palmer did just that, holding the fresh eggs he had gathered from his chicken coop in one hand while enjoying the fantastic sky show.

The fresh mountain air around him had a sharp morning bite to it even though it was in the middle of the summer. And the smell of pine felt extra thick this morning. By the afternoon, the smell would be of hot pine, something he loved just as much.

In fact, if he admitted it to himself, he loved everything about living in the high mountains of central Idaho. The mornings were crisp and then the day would warm up nice, leaving enough heat in the evenings to make sitting on the big log porch looking out over the Payette River comfortable.

In the winter he thought of the snow as a protective blanket, white and beautiful and covering everything.

At one point, before the event that killed most everyone, the End of Time Bar had been a beautiful log home perched on a bluff overlooking the river. Five bedrooms and a massive open area with a huge fireplace on the main floor. He had found it while trying to get away from the smell of all the people who had died suddenly in Boise.

And everywhere else in the world it seemed.

No one had been here in this cabin, but the pantry was stocked and the freezer was full and there was a generator and a back-up generator that worked fine after the power finally shut off three months later.

And he had little doubt the previous owners were dead somewhere. Most everyone was dead that he knew, including his wife, his parents, everyone at Boise State University where he had taught in the law school.

Everyone.

And after a few days of wandering around in a state of shock, he realized he needed to find a place away from all the rotting death.

He had headed north into the mountains, walking, following the two-lane road toward central Idaho.

He had seen the big log home on the bluff through the trees from the road. After he realized it would be perfect for him to get through the winter, he raided other nearby cabins and went into Cascade to get supplies and then just stayed put for the winter until the smell of millions of dead finally faded.

He still hadn't been back down to Boise in the last five years since everyone died. He had no desire to see his home in the north end of town, his wife's remains in their living room, his friends all dead. He had no idea why he had survived, but another survivor he had met said it was because he had been in a bank vault.

It seemed that everyone who had survived had been underground or in something like a vault.

Palmer had gone into the bank to put some papers in his safe deposit box and when he came out everyone was dead.

He didn't remember much about those first days other than not knowing what to do with his wife's body. He had finally covered her with her favorite blanket and just left.

By the time the first spring rolled around, he discovered that other survivors had come into the mountains for the same reason he had. They were in cabins all over the area.

So one day while sitting all alone in the big living room area, he decided all the survivors needed a place to gather and what better place than a bar.

So he opened up the End of Time. He put a sign down on the road pointing up the hill that said, "End of Time Bar, Saloon, and Eatery. Open every day from eleven until past dark."

He lived upstairs and for a long time no one showed up. Then a couple from a few miles away stopped by and that got the word spreading.

It took most of the next year for the word to spread through the entire area and up into the more remote mountains, but during the second summer more and more survivors came out of their hiding.

And now most afternoons and evenings a good twenty people would be in the place, talking, pretending that everyone they had loved wasn't dead, and just going on with life.

He didn't take money for drinks or food, just exchange. And that kept his pantry full, his freezers stocked with venison, fish, and other game, and his liquor shelves full.

And he often had help in the kitchen when someone came up with a nifty idea for a new dish. Or something they had learned from their mother.

Some days it was hard to remember the old world, the old life.

Most of the time he didn't want to remember.

Three years after the event he heard about how survivors from all over the country were starting up four major new cities and Portland, Oregon, was one of them. He thought about heading there, but finally decided to just stay and run his little bar and restaurant.

And most of the others who lived in the cabins up and down the valley along the river did the same.

Now, after two years, the road from Boise up through Idaho had been cleared by a crew from Portland and his bar and restaurant were major stops along the way for anyone traveling through. Instead of people walking up the road to his place, most everyone had a motorcycle or an ATV or a truck. He had to clear out some brush for a parking lot last summer.

It seems his place had a real reputation for good food, fun conversation, and strong drinks.

He kind of liked that.

More than he wanted to admit.

So Monday morning was going along great. He had the eggs from the chicken coop in the fridge and the bread was finished baking, filling the huge log home with a rich thick buttery smell that felt like it could make a person fat just by breathing in too much of it.

He had fried himself two eggs and cut some hot, fresh bread and had just turned to take his coffee and his breakfast out to the tables on the log porch when she appeared.

She didn't come through any door.

She just appeared.

In front of the river-rock fireplace, among the wooden tables and chairs that filled the large area.

She was smiling, but with a worried look in her large brown eyes.

He just shook his head and stared at her.

Not possible.

She had short brown hair, cut close. Her face was round, with wide brown eyes. She looked to be about five-six with a thin frame. She wore jeans, tennis shoes, and a summer blouse with a sports bra showing through the blouse.

She was the best-looking woman he had seen since the world ended. A lot of women had come through here over the last five years, sometimes with other women, sometimes with men, sometimes even alone.

None had taken his breath away like this one.

And he felt like he had met her before. Not possible. He was sure he would remember, but it felt like he had.

Or he had dreamed about her.

How in the hell had she done that magic appearing trick?

He glanced back at the heavy wood front door. Still closed solidly.

He hadn't opened the slider yet to the porch, and she sure as hell didn't look like Santa Claus coming down the big river-rock fireplace.

So that made her a magician or a ghost. He was hoping for a magician. He didn't want his wonderful home and business to be haunted.

He looked down at the eggs and bread on the plate in his hand, then back at her.

Her eyes were wide and she was clearly worried about his reaction to her suddenly just being there.

Damn she looked familiar.

But after seeing the entire world die around him, he was beyond most reactions.

"I suppose you came for some breakfast," he said. "I don't normally serve breakfast, but I'll be glad to make you some."

He was surprised his voice stayed level and calm.

She now looked surprised, which made her even more beautiful.

Amazing that since Cindie had died, he hadn't thought much about any other women. They had gotten married in his last year of law school and he had only been teaching for two years when she and everyone died.

He missed her, a great deal the first few years, but sadly he didn't think of her often these days. He had blocked off that living part of his life. He called it "before" when talking about it.

He turned and put his plate on the big island that divided the kitchen from the big room and went around.

"Eggs, bread, coffee?" he asked.

She still just stood there, but she nodded.

"If you are not a ghost, come and sit while I cook."

He pointed to one of the barstools at the counter facing the kitchen.

She nodded and moved toward the stool directly on the other side of the counter from him.

"Two eggs or three?" he asked, opening up the fridge.

"Just two, thank you, professor," she said.

Her voice was low and level, but he could still feel the nervousness in it. And then it dawned on him what she had said. Around here no one knew his history. He was just Palmer.

No last name, nothing.

Just Palmer.

But this woman who had appeared like a ghost out of nowhere clearly knew of his past.

What the hell was going on?

"Just Palmer," he said, turning back to get the eggs while he got his nerves under control.

"And what is your name? Or should I just call you Ghost?"

She laughed and he loved the sound of that. He loved how she looked, her wide brown eyes, and her smile. And he now was certain he knew her.

Or he had to be still in bed dreaming.

No other explanation that he could logically think of.

"Ghost would actually be nice," she said, "but my real name is Marissa Warren."

For some reason he wanted to put a "Doctor" in front of her name, but he didn't say anything. He had no idea where that came from either.

After five years, maybe he was losing his mind.

He started the eggs cooking, then without turning around asked how she wanted them.

"Over easy," she said.

He turned and slid his plate in front of her. "That's what those are. Eat those before they get cold while I fix these."

She nodded as he slid her silverware and turned back to the stove.

He couldn't let himself look too much at her or he would lose all sense of anything. And right now he needed to figure out just what in the world was going on.

He pretended to just focus on the cooking while he took deep, slow breaths to calm.

After a moment she said, "Wow, this bread is wonderful."

"Thank you," he said. "Taught to me by a fellow who lives up by the old stibnite mining town. He comes down a few times a year, camps out in the trees down the river. I built an outhouse down there for those who want to stay overnight."

"And the eggs are perfect," she said. "I didn't realize how hungry I was."

"Mountain air will do that to you," he said, finishing up the eggs he was cooking and then cutting off another piece of bread.

He put his plate on the counter directly across from her and started to eat, standing there, half watching her finish eating.

Where did he know her from? Had she been one of his students? Was that where?

But there was no doubt she was stunning, just flat stunning.

And he was attracted to her, more than he wanted to be.

A lot more than he wanted to be.

Finally she looked up at him and he felt like a deer under a spotlight, frozen by her wonderful brown eyes.

"You're not shocked at me just appearing?" she asked after a moment.

"I watched the entire world and everyone I knew and loved die five years ago," he said. "So I don't shock easily, but I am wondering how you got in here. Ghost or magician?"

She nodded and sat back, smiling. "Neither. You ever watch the old *Star Trek* television show?"

"Sure, all the time," he said, laughing. "So you are telling me you beamed in from a spaceship? I didn't hear the transporter music."

She laughed, but then nodded. "Seems we forgot to cue the music for me this morning."

He didn't know whether to laugh or to run screaming for the door. But something was triggering in his memory now. A dream he had had back right after everyone died, about being on a spaceship and then being put back.

He had assumed that dream was caused by the same thing that had killed everyone

---

More Seeders Universe Stories
Available at your favorite booksellers.

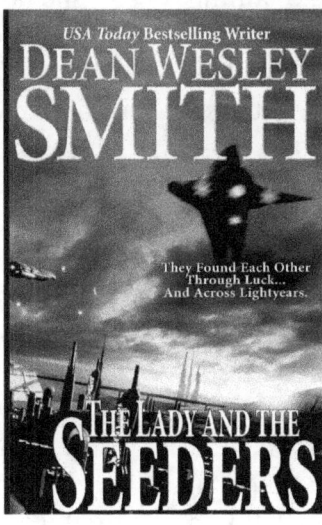

and had just put it out of his mind, even though it had been very, very vivid.

But now he remembered where he had met her. She had been on the spaceship in his dream.

Holy crap!

"So you one of the aliens who killed everyone?" he asked, keeping as calm as he could.

She seemed startled for a moment, then she laughed. "Nope, I'm as human as you are. And what killed everyone was an electromagnetic pulse that came in from space and just shorted out human brains and a lot of animal brains as well."

"The reason all survivors were in vaults or underground," Palmer said, nodding.

She nodded. "Over one million people around the world survived that first wave."

"So why did you take all of us to your spaceships and then put us back into the death?"

She nodded. "So you do remember? I figured because of your genes you would."

He nodded. He was remembering more and more by the minute. He could now see the large meeting room full of smelly survivors, all shocked, looking down at the planet below.

He remembered a man explaining that they were rescuing all the survivors off the entire planet because another electromagnetic wave was coming. That over a thousand ships would take the survivors out of harms way and then return them so they could start rebuilding their home.

And he remembered her, giving medical care to people in the room, working with a smile and wonderful manner.

He remembered watching her until she approached him and they had talked for a few minutes, then she had moved on.

"There are still four large ships in orbit over this planet trying to help in the recovery," she said. "All are human. Actually, a branch of humanity called Seeders. We all have a special gene. Most humans do not, but you do, which allows you to remember the time on the ship."

"So why did you come back?"

She actually blushed slightly and looked down at her empty plate.

Then she looked up. "I was on one of the ships that left after the rescue. I had a mission on another planet to complete that took me three years. Then I asked to come back here because I wanted to see how you were doing."

"Me?" he asked, shocked.

And now he felt embarrassed.

She nodded and the silence filled the space between them for a moment.

Finally she broke it.

"I really love the life you have built here," she said, "and when we met again I didn't want to lie to you and pretend to be a survivor. So I got permission after almost a year of asking to just transport in directly to see if you would remember me."

"You are very hard to forget," he said, smiling at her. "But I have to admit in all that trauma, I wrote off that short time on the ship and meeting you as a dream."

She nodded to that.

"Are you a doctor?"

"I am," she said. "At least what passes for one in the advanced Seeders worlds."

He shook his head. "You'll have to explain that to me later."

She smiled and her entire face lit up and the smile reached those fantastic eyes. "I would be glad to."

"So, Ghost, how about we take our coffee and go out on the porch and enjoy the morning," he said. "You can enjoy my world while telling me about yours."

Her smile got bigger, if that was possible.

"I would love that very much."

And three hours later, after telling him some pretty amazing stories, he asked her if she wanted to stay for lunch and she said she did.

And she said she would pay her way by helping him. Together they got things ready for lunch and then while he cooked she waited on the twelve people who showed up. He introduced her as Ghost from Portland and everyone liked her right off.

She fit in perfectly with her bright smile and wonderful laugh.

It was everything he could do to not stare at her instead of cooking.

And who knew a doctor from space could carry four plates of hot food at the same time.

He was going to have to ask her where exactly in space she learned that skill.

No doubt it had been a strange Monday. But when you serve food and drinks at the End of Time, things like today have to be expected.

The Latest Seeders Universe Novel
now available from all your favorite booksellers in trade paperback and ebook editions.

USA TODAY BESTSELLING AUTHOR

DEAN WESLEY SMITH

STARBURST

A SEEDERS UNIVERSE NOVEL

USA TODAY BESTSELLING AUTHOR

DEAN WESLEY SMITH

KILLING

THE **TOP 10**

Sacred Cows

Indie

OF PUBLISHING

A WMG WRITER'S GUIDE

As indie publishing flourishes, many, many myths form around this new boom-ing area of publishing. USA Today *bestselling author and major indie blogger Dean Wesley Smith takes a cut at killing some of the myths before they can take root.*

From the myth that indie writers can't get books into bookstores (they can) to the idea that indie publishing must be easy (it is and it isn't), Dean knocks ten myths down one after another and might just save you years of wasted time.

Author of the acclaimed Killing the Top Ten Sacred Cows of Publishing, *this com-panion WMG Writer's Guide for indie writers and publishers will become a necessity for your reference shelf.*

Killing the Top Ten Sacred Cows of Indie Publishing
A WMG Writer's Guide

Part 2 of 2

Sacred Cow #6
I Can Put a Book Up for Sale and Leave It There Forever

or conversely...
if I put a book up for sale,
I have to change it every week

THIS DOUBLE-HEADED myth is a real killer to income and books.

A paraphrased conversation I had with a friend sort of sums up this myth.

A friend of mine said, "Joe Konrath says that as indie writers, we must tend our gardens."

I agreed, but added, "And we need to learn when to leave the garden alone to grow as well."

I have heard both sides of this myth a lot, and I'm sure early on in this new indie world, I advocated one side or the other a few times myself, more than likely far more than a few times.

Now I advocate walking a line on balance.

Some History

For a century and more, books had no staying power, for the most part. There were always books that survived in the used and rare world. Sure. But rarely did a book outside that world survive in any fashion, with a few exceptions.

The exceptions were the very, very unusual books that found new readers generation after generation and that publishers kept the books in print.

In modern publishing, those books tended to be classics, or young adult books. In fact, for a few decades, the backlist (older books) in young adult sold better than the front list (new books put out that year).

Sadly, very, very few genre books were kept in print for very long. Even classics and major award winners are lost and out of print, unless brought back into print by a small press.

But the publishers of those books that had a long life were doing what indie writers need to learn to do. Every four or five years, they would put on an updated new cover, or reissue the book with some sort of fanfare, or some other new promotion. (Note: I said every few years, not every other month.)

But for the majority of all books published in the last century, the print runs were either limited, or the book was considered disposable.

The disposable aspect of books came from two major places. First came World War Two, where paperbacks were included as supplies to the soldiers to be read and passed around and then tossed away. Second, publishers started to just ask for covers back of many books in the returns system to save on shipping, so the bookstores would strip the covers and get credit for the unsold books.

After decades, books to traditional publishers became like bananas on a fruit stand. If they didn't sell quickly, they spoiled and thus were destroyed, put out of print, and forgotten.

Books became produce. (And sadly, to traditional publishers, they still are. Plus they have become assets of a corporate balance sheet even if they are out of print or only for sale in a bad and expensive electronic edition.)

Up until the last five years or so, and the rise of the electronic book, this was the feelings for books *and how authors felt about them as well.*

I can't believe how many times I heard from authors in traditional publishing that you were only as good as your last book. (I'm sure I said that myself a few times along the way, and I believed it because I worked in traditional publishing.)

So this idea that indie writers now have books they can publish and keep in print for a long time is great. But they publish it and then what do they do? And here comes this duel-sided myth.

Indie writers tend to fall into two crazy camps.

Camp One: They put the book up and change the price weekly and the cover monthly.

Camp Two: They put the book up and forget it.

There is a balance point in the center of the two camps, which is where the analogy of tending a garden comes in perfectly.

Indie writers, in this case, must learn from how traditional publishers treated classics and bestselling young adult books. The traditional publishers kept those books alive and selling for decades.

Indie writers can do the same thing if they know what they are doing.

The Silliness of Both Sides

To start off, you must learn to look at books with a long view into the future. Very few writers do this.

Very, very few.

Almost no writer I know looks at books as an invetment that could pay off over decades.

So let me use the "tend the garden" analogy to show the two extremes.

The Care-Too-Much problem.

You plant some corn seeds in your garden. (That's publishing your book to be clear.)

Come back the next day, nothing is happening to the seeds in your garden, so you give them more water, sit in the window watching, nothing happens, water it more, watch more.

Nothing.

On day three, since there is nothing happening yet, you decide you must have planted the seeds in the wrong place, so you dig up the seeds and move them, give them more water, plant them again.

Sit and watch for something to happen. Maybe you put the seeds too deep, so you dig them up again and bring them right to the surface.

Watch. Two days later nothing.

You panic.

So you dig the seeds up again and bury them deeper because you read on a blog somewhere that's what you should do.

And on and on and on.

You get the picture I hope. Books are like corn. They are not magic, they take time to find an audience. Books take time to grow an audience.

So what about the other side of this? The Put The Book Up and Forget Problem.

You decide to plant corn in your garden. You plant the seeds. (Again this is publishing a book.)

You walk away from your garden and go back to work and don't even bother to water anything or weed anything. In six months or a year or two you look at it again and the corn is dead, buried under weeds.

Note that neither extreme works well.

Most indie writers I have met are the first example, not giving anything time to grow or live, messing with it all the time.

I tend to fall in the second camp far too much because of my training that books are written and then gone. So I plant seeds and forget them and do nothing to help anything along.

Both sides of this myth do not produce good LONG TERM product year after year.

A Way Out of the Two-Sided Myth

Perspective is the way to the center from both sides of this myth.

And continuing to learn about how book buyers find books helps as well.

So using Kris and myself as an example here, and what I did when electronic books got started, let me show you some aspects of both sides, and the problems of both sides.

Way back when Kindle first opened the KDP program, a friend taught a number of other writers and me how to get books onto Kindle and Smashwords. (I have detailed in other places how I slowly came to realize how my backlist, with this new system, was a gold mine waiting to be tapped.)

So as with most things I do, I jumped in and went to work. My attitude back then was I needed to get as many titles up as I could as fast as I could.

It was just me doing all the work, and I was putting up my own stories and Kris's short stories and then eventually we started putting up some backlist novels.

And one and a half years later, I had over 200 titles up on Kindle, Smashwords, and B&N.

I had not gone back and looked at a one of them. Just put the book or story up and moved to the next one.

After a year and a half, the books were making enough money that we could hire some fulltime help. Since we had started a major publishing company once before (Pulphouse Publishing in 1987), we knew where this was heading, so we created a corporation and found the best person to run the business.

All paid for because I had pushed over 200 plus titles up and left them alone.

Allyson Longueira came on board and after looking at everything for a month and getting herself up to speed, she came to me and Kris and said simply, "We need to change everything, every cover, everything we have up so far. And we need to reproof everything and redo all the blurbs."

In other words, I had paid no attention to the garden and it was covered in weeds and the income was about to be choked off if we didn't do some weeding and new planting and repairing.

You see, my covers sucked. I had done them in PowerPoint quickly. And the blurbs I hadn't paid the slightest bit of attention to, and proofing was lax on those early books. We often used the traditional publisher printed versions of our stories and those, as are most traditional published books, were riddled with mistakes.

Allyson was right. At the two-year mark after I started putting stuff up as fast as I could, we needed to tend that garden.

Desperately.

She started fixing things, and we put up some new books as well, and we started working on the old blurbs and took off the worst offending covers fairly quickly. By the time she had been with us for six months, our title count was up to 250 titles, and she wasn't a quarter of the way through fixing the old stuff.

But the garden was starting to look better at least.

And the income was increasing, especially since the new work we put up was much better in look, blurbs, and proofing.

And readers of indie books were starting to expect better at this point in indie publishing and we were shifting to give it to them.

The extra money coming in allowed us to hire more help in WMG Publishing. About a year after hiring Allyson, we had enough to start the audio department as well.

After one year, we had managed to fix all but a few of those early titles I had done quickly, and our title count was over 300 titles.

That's a very large garden, let me tell you.

Now, another year plus has past, we are over 400 titles and climbing, and almost all but a very few have been touched and fixed from those early days. And many of the first changes Allyson did when she started have also been changed out again.

We have branded the covers and books on the major series and are in the process of branding to series and to genre the minor series as well.

We have a proofreader on staff, a full-time promotions person coming on board in a month, and a second and third sales team members coming on board this fall.

Now understand, when I say the word "we" in that above story, it's not me anymore doing much besides writing checks. Sure, I do *Smith's Monthly* covers and layout and I help edit *Fiction River* and that's it.

In fact, right now I spend most of my daylight time working on online work-shops, which I love and keep me learning.

Kris and I do not run WMG Publishing and haven't now for more than a year. Allyson is the publisher, we call her the boss, and she runs the business and the seven or eight employees and works with the authors in *Fiction River* and so on.

Kris and I created an indie/traditional publisher hybrid.

Honestly, many bestselling authors who are leaving publishing are doing the same sorts of things in various forms, hiring help for many aspects that are needed in this new indie world.

Kris and I let the money coming from the indie publishing build the business. We plowed every cent back into the growth. And we still are.

In other words, we are investing our income in our future.

So now our garden is well-tended, unlike what it was back three years ago. It is expanding every month as Kris and I continue to add in new backlist and keep writing new front list books and stories as well. I would imagine our title count will be past five hundred by the end of 2014.

And *Fiction River* has brought in many other authors and editors and WMG has plans to expand into many new projects as time and money allow.

How did we do this? Honestly, we found a balance between leaving the garden alone and spending too much time on every title.

At four hundred plus titles, we can't pay attention to every title, and yes, some get forgotten for a time, so we still lean a little too much to the put-up-and-forget side of things. But that will be changing a lot as 2014 goes on.

Suggestions to Find a Balance

The WIBBOW test was coined by professional writer Scott William Carter. WIBBOW stands for:

Would I Be Better Off Writing?

For indie writers, the answer is almost always yes. As I discovered as I pounded up over 200 different backlist titles from Kris and my decades of writing, new product sells old product.

The best promotion is always the next book.

But covers must be tended to and as your knowledge grows about covers, you must fix covers every three or four year. Sometimes genre trends just move in looks. You need to stay abreast of the changes. (That takes research time as well.)

As you get better at writing sales copy instead of plot summaries, your blurbs need to be fixed.

To get the book in the right place, you also need to keep learning genre. That's critical to sales.

And then there is that ugly topic of pricing, which I will talk about in the 9th Sacred Cows of Indie Publishing coming up shortly.

So here are my suggestions to find a balance, since I have been in this since the beginning of this crazy movement, and also spent decades in traditional publishing.

Publish the book with the best modern-looking cover to genre you can do, with the best blurb, and with luck in the right spot in the bookstores.

Get the book into as many places as you can, from Kindle to Kobo to B&N to iBooks to Smashwords to audio to paper editions. Everywhere. You must try to find as many readers as you can.

Tell your social media, your friends, your family, get it to a few bloggers, and other minor promotions you may do, and that's it. WIBBOW test.

Go back to writing. Write the next book. DO NOT TOUCH THE PREVIOUS BOOK.

Check your sales every month at the end of the month. Not sales numbers, but income from that book. Let me say that

again. Track INCOME. You need to track what each book (title) is making you per month total from all the sites. (TrackerBox program can do this for you.)

After one year, look at the sales figures for each of your titles. If one title is not selling hardly at all, time to take a look at it. Check first the location on the shelf, the genre. Have a friend read it and see if your idea of the genre matches your friend's. If it does, then look at the blurb. If it is full of plot and passive verbs, learn how to rewrite that into sales language. Then have someone look at your cover and tell you the truth about it. Somehow who knows commercial book covers.

Fix what needs to be fixed on all under performing titles, and go back to writing. In other words, tend the garden and let things continue to grow.

With every title, novel, short story, or collection, check the sales after one year to see if they are on track.

In the next chapter of *Killing the Top Ten Sacred Cows of Indie Publishing*, I talk about the myth of small sales numbers. So that will help you understand how to judge when a book is selling well and when it is under performing and needs tending.

SUMMARY

This myth can really kill sales and entire writer's careers.

On one side, the example of waiting for growth every few days in a garden, the myth can cause extreme disappointment. And frustration. And it can kill writing of new projects and titles.

The other side of putting up and ignoring doesn't allow your books to change with the times, doesn't allow you to follow under-performing titles, and flat isn't good business when you have a valuable property.

Each title is a property. Remember that. Putting the title up and ignoring it for too long would be like building a house and then just letting it sit, not doing anything to it to keep it up. It might be fine for a time, but eventually it will need work and repair.

So find a balance between too much change on a title and too little change.

But my biggest suggestion to everyone is think of publishing as a long-term business.

Think in units of years, not units of days.

Give readers time to find your work, to read your work, to enjoy your work.

Tend your garden. But don't overwater it on one side, or let the weeds and lack of care choke it out on the other.

Find a balance.

And have fun.

Sacred Cow #7
I Have to Sell a Lot of Copies Very Quickly or My Book is a Failure

OF COURSE, THIS shows no understanding of property and long-term return on investment. But most writers wouldn't know that, so they get trapped in this thinking all the time.

And when expectations of sales do not match actual sales, writers often quit writing, or make really silly decisions like lowering prices for no good business or promotion reason. When decisions are

made out of panic that a book isn't selling up to some made-up expectation, then nothing but problems arise.

Some History

Interestingly enough, this myth is based solidly out of the way traditional publishers think. And for a bunch of indie writers who pride themselves in thinking and acting differently, following traditional publishing thinking in this makes me shake my head in wonder.

First:

For the last thirty or so years, traditional publishers tracked the success or failure quickly of a book, not on how many sold at first, but on books shipped. And if a book didn't ship up to expectations (meaning orders placed ahead of the book's ship date didn't match a made-up number on a profit-and-loss sheet), then the book was deemed a failure and quickly dropped out of print.

And the author would have an awful time selling more books under that author name.

Second:

Bestseller lists for traditional publishers relied on a combination of books shipped and books sold in certain stores in a week-long period. So if that book didn't sell quickly and in large numbers, the book didn't make a bestseller list.

Third:

With very few exceptions, traditional publishers for thirty or more years considered books to be like produce at a grocery store. There was limited shelf space, so if a book didn't sell, it was destroyed and the covers returned for credit, or if it was a hardback, the entire book was shipped back to the publisher for credit.

For the longest time, returns under 50% were considered good sales and returns over 50% in a short period of time, the book was a failure.

So here comes indie publishing, with the ability to think long term, unlike traditional publishers. Indie publishers can plan sales on a book for a ten-year or twenty-year plan.

Traditional publishers flat can't do that with the quarterly demand of profits for their corporate masters. They must churn the profit, kill books that don't sell quickly, and move on to the next book.

This chapter I hope will give a few indie publishers a different perspective on sales. But that myth that has come from traditional publishers (that books must sell a lot and very quickly) is a very, very deep and hard myth to crack for most.

Some Math:
First Traditional Publishing

In this world at the moment, if you sold a genre book to a traditional publisher and got a $4,000 advance, you would be expected to sell about 3,000 copies in six months total before it vanished and dropped into the weed-filled garden (see last post) of electronic book sales just dripping along.

3,000 initial sales. That's after returns and I assume you are smart enough if you are reading this to not have an agent taking a piece of that $4,000.

Let's make one more assumption: None of your sales are to high discount stores.

So you would get 6% of the $7.99 cover price per sale for the mass market paper. Or about 48 cents per sale for paper.

For electronic sales you would get 25% of net. Publisher puts it up at $7.99 electronic. That's about $1.40 per sale. ($7.99 x 70% x 25%)

Half of the 3,000 copies to be successful for this book are electronic sales, half are paper sales.

Paper: 1,500 sales x $.48 = $720

Electronic 1,500 sales x $1.40 = $2,100

Your book earned out $2,820 of the $4,000 advance.

The $4,000 is all the money you will ever see on that genre book.

Let me be generous and say it took only three years from the moment you wrote the book to the book became a wilted piece of produce to the publisher. (Chances are it took closer to four years, but let's go with three.)

And remember, you won't get that book back. It will continue to trickle sales in electronic form (because the publisher won't care anymore, the book is just out there, so the garden for that book is not being tended). And at 25% of net, you might as well just forget that book until you can get the copyright reverted at 35 years.

Indie Publisher Math

I'm going to make some major assumptions here. I am going to assume that you have a paper edition of your book and you have your book available in all the different major online bookstores direct so you are getting paid monthly.

So in electronic editions, you price your novel at $6.99. (Below what your traditional publisher would have priced it.) So you will be making approximately $4.90 per sale

In paper you price your book so that in the extended distribution you get at least $2.00 per sale.

You put your book up in all electronic venues (Kindle, B&N, iBooks, Kobo,

GooglePlay, Smashwords, and so on), and your book sells 20 copies the first month total across all sites.

And 5 copies in paper the first month.

So in one month your income is $108.00. ($98.00 electronic plus $10 paper.) And you are thinking your book is a failure after the first month.

I am going to be making another assumption. I am going to assume that as time goes on, every year or two, you tend your garden. (See Chapter Six.)

So over the next few months, your book sales grow slightly, but then they come down some toward the end of the first year, so that you are averaging over the entire first year of the book being in print the 25 sales per month.

So in that first year you made ($108.00 x 12) $1,296.00

In the same three years at that rate, without you doing much but some minor tending of the garden, you will have made $3,888.00.

More WMG Writers' Guides
from all your favorite booksellers
in trade paper and electronic editions.

Almost exactly in the same amount of time, the same amount of money you would have made in traditional publishing.

Only difference is that you still have the book and it's still earning for you into the future, where with traditional you don't own it anymore and won't for a very long time.

25 copies sales per month.

At that level, it's a book that many indie publishers would think is a complete failure.

I won't even go into the million things you could do to help the sales of that book, such as writing more books, writing more books in the same world, learning how to do better covers and switch the cover out in a couple of years, and so on.

Yeah, a success selling it to traditional publishing for $4,000 dollars, but a failure at 25 copies sales per month?

And that's this myth.

Look at the Difference in Sales Numbers

The traditional publisher managed to shove out 3,000 copies of the book, half electronic, half paper, and still didn't come close to earning you back your $4,000 advance.

You ended up with almost the same amount of money by selling 720 electronic copies total in three years and 180 copies in paper in three years.

But you will, even at that pace, eventually sell the 1,500 copies of the electronic books in just over six years and the full 1,500 copies of the paper in around twenty or so years assuming your paper sales do not increase over time.

And when you end up with that amount of sales on the book, you will have made on that book ($4.90 x 1,500) $7,350 electronic and $3,000 paper.

Over $10,000 total and you will still own and can be selling the book into the future.

So Why Do Indie Publishers Hold Onto this Myth?

Basically, we all want our books to sell well, have a lot of fans, and hope that it gets read everywhere. That's just common sense.

But the problem arises when a book doesn't sell as well as "expected" and the indie publisher starts making bad decisions about the book.

So what is "expected?"

I like the average of 25 sales per month over all platforms. I like that expectation, and it allows me to have great fun when something jumps with more sales. And after a year or so, if book isn't selling to that "expected" average, it's time to tend the garden.

That's my expectation. But I know a ton of indie writers who would think that expectation far, far too low.

The statement those indie writers say to me is this: "I want to make a living with my writing within five years. I can't do that with sales like that."

Sadly, I just laugh when someone says that to me, and I really shouldn't. As I said before, this is a tough myth to crack.

Making a Living...More Math

Start with the amount needed to make a living. Let's just use a nice round number like $40,000 gross income. Low, but not too low. You pick your own number.

You know that every novel you are going to put up will have an average income of about $1,296 per year selling 25 copies total per month across all platforms, including paper. (Average means some books will sell more, some less, but average over all your titles.)

So take $40,000.00 and divide by $1,296.00 and you get the number 30. Thirty novels to be making $40,000 per year in five years.

5 years into 30 novels means you need to write 6 novels per year. One every-other-month.

I CAN'T DO THAT! (I hear the screams...)

Wow, that's sad you are stuck in that myth as well. Don't you folks watch my Writing in Public blog every day?

So to the math...

250 words is one manuscript page for this discussion.

A novel is 80,000 words long for this discussion.

80,000 words divided by 250 words is 320 pages for the novel.

You have 60 days in two months. So to do around 320 pages in two months, you must average around 5 pages per day.

Most writers I know do about 4 pages in an hour, so that means you need to spend generously 1.5 hours per day writing to be making a living with your writing in five years.

And then, if you kept writing, the amount of money you make would just keep going up every year.

So your books sell horribly by your expected standards. You only sell 25 copies in a month of your most recent novel.

Write six books a year and you'll be making a nice living even with your books selling horribly.

Unless, of course, you let the thinking from traditional publishing into the picture and start making bad decisions or get depressed and stop writing. Then you won't make a living in writing in five years. You'll just be bitter and sad and will have lost a dream, all because you let this myth get into your head.

Sadly, I've watched that with a bunch of indie writers around me already.

Quick Side Note on Investing

For those of you who understand investing, I did an entire lecture in the lecture series on thinking of writing as an investment.

Using this math, let me show you quickly how that works and if you want more about this way of thinking, take that lecture.

First question is: What is my investment in the book?

Some round numbers...100 hours of writing. 10 hours of production. 10 hours of misc promotion. 120 hours of time per novel. Figure your time is worth $20.00 per hour to you have $2,400 in time.

Set costs...Copyediting (proofing) about $400. Art and misc costs $200 to make this simple.

Total costs are $3,000 per book (counting your time at $20 per hour.)

Most investors are happy with a 10% return on investment per year.

Your book is a $3,000 investment. To make a 10% investment return on your book, you need to sell $300 per year. Far, far under that $1,296.00 sales number at 25 copies.

In fact, selling six copies total per month would get you a 10% return on your investment.

Just another way to try to get some perspective on this myth that your book needs to sell a lot of copies quickly.

Sure, we all want that. But those of us with some perspective can do just fine with sales just chugging right along slowly.

Publishing As a Long Game

When I got serious about my writing finally and found Heinlein's Rules in 1982 and really started writing and learning, I hoped to be making a living with my writing in ten years.

And I purposely kept my expenses on the bottom. I drove an old used car and worked only as much as I needed to work my day jobs so that I had more time to write. As it turned out, it took me about five years, but even then I was adding to my early writing income with editing and publishing gigs.

I was lucky to make it in five years and I knew it. I'm not counting the seven years before that where I was lost in the rewriting myths. But if you count from my first sale, it's twelve years.

Indie writers who are in a hurry make bad decisions. Publishing on both sides of this fence is a long game.

SUMMARY
Suggestions to Help With this Myth

1...Always be focused on writing the next book.

2...Do what you can to promote when you release a book, but watch your time. Writing the next book is far more important in the long run.

3...Have a five or ten year plan and then work your writing schedule into it. If you really can't spend an hour a day at your writing, (barring major life events) than maybe you should not be thinking about making a living. Nothing at all wrong with writing being your love, not your living.

4...Keep learning how to become a better storyteller. Writing more entertaining books tends to bring more sales.

5...Do all the standard stuff to help your sales, such as having a publisher name and a publisher web site as well as an author web site. Do a newsletter and some social media, but again watch your time.

6...Only look at your numbers every month and no more often. Then don't worry about book sales numbers, just write down how much each title (book) has earned you each month.

7...Do not change anything about a book, the cover, the blurbs, nothing. Only allow yourself to change something at the year anniversary of the book being published. And if it is selling at the base level you hope to have, leave the book alone and look at it in another year.

8...Make sure you are staying abreast of all changes and keep your books in as many markets as you can directly.

9...When life knocks you down, which it will do almost every year, climb back on and just keep going. Five year or ten year plan will have many failures and missed months along the way. Adjust as you go and don't quit.

10...Focus on writing the next book.

The key with this myth is to ignore what is coming at you from other writers about speed of sales. And move away from traditional publishing produce thinking that if your book doesn't sell quickly it will spoil.

Make your five-year business plan and set your expectations.

If you have only one book up, selling 25 copies per month is unrealistic. Don't expect it. *And hoping to be lucky is not a business plan.*

But if you have a bunch of novels out and you are in the second year, selling 25 copies average across your titles is realistic. It might not happen, but it is worth aiming for.

Plus, if you also write short stories, they can help. Collections sell pretty well. Not as well as novels, but they can help in the total income.

Stop looking at sales numbers and hoping for huge sales numbers.

Plan for five or ten years out and focus on writing the next book.

And have fun.

Sacred Cow #8
I Have Missed My Chance

...or in similar thinking...
I am so far behind, why bother starting?

THIS MYTH, OF course, has a lot of origins, but the biggest one is the totally false thinking that this indie world is a gold rush. Nope. It's not anymore. Indie publishing is now a new part of publishing here to stay for any foreseeable future.

And it might, if some people are correct, become the dominant form of publishing. Who knows.

Some History

Most people think that indie publishing has only been around now since Amazon one fine day opened its doors in the KDP program.

(snort)

Sorry, I have a really hard time even keeping a straight face with that kind of statement. It shows a complete lack of understanding of the publishing business.

Fact: Indie publishing (formally called small press publishing) has been around in publishing since the beginning of publishing in this modern world, which means clear back to the start of the United States and even before.

Kris and I started an indie (small press) publisher in 1987 called Pulphouse Publishing. And we did POD printing for our books, worked with a small bindery, and sold to bookstores just like the big traditional publishers did.

So indie publishing has been around a very, very long time.

Edger Rice Burroughs started an indie press in 1923 to publish his own books. (It is still in existence, by the way. Called Edger Rice Burroughs Inc. Now that's some future planning.)

But this new world that has made it very, very possible for writers with no knowledge of the publishing business to get their books to readers directly. That ability for nonprofessional writers has only been around since the KDP program started up.

Those early few years of this new wave happened fast, first with the KDP program, followed by Smashwords, and then B&N opening up their bookstores. That was followed by the POD programs to get paper into regular bookstores. All those changes happened seemingly instantly and every indie publisher seemed to be in a huge hurry.

We were no exception to that in those first few years. It felt like a gold rush, no doubt.

But then everything settled. The explosive growth of electronic books has slowed to a tiny and healthy growth. We are now in a new normal.

Granted, there are major changes coming in publishing because of disruptive technology hitting big companies not capable of handling the changes. But for indie publishers, we are now playing on a level field with all traditional publishers.

But I'm Behind!

My questions to you, if you are feeling that you are behind are this?

"Who are you behind and when did it become a race?"

I know Kris and I are sure not racing anyone. We have our business plan, we are staying out of all debt, and putting up new tittles as we can. Our pace, WMG Publishing Inc. pace, is just our pace. We are not in a race with anyone.

And to be honest, other than to learn from other indie publishers, we don't care what others do. If someone does something that makes sense for us and seems to work, we might try it when the time is right.

We don't try to chase any fad or stay even with anyone.

We just do what we do.

The problem with this myth about being behind is that it causes writers to just not start.

It's easier to just sit and feel sorry for yourself that you missed some imaginary boat than to actually make a business plan and start.

On the door of my office I have a sign that is a quote that I have no idea who said it and don't really care to look it up.

I see it every single time I walk into my writing office. There is a reason it is on my office door.

The sign says, "...there are two kinds of people in this world, those who wish and those who will, and the world and its goods will always belong to those who will."

How to Get Out of the Feeling of Being Behind

—First off, stop comparing yourself to other people.

Look around at what other indie publishers are doing and learn and adopt ideas that work for you and ignore all the rest.

—Ask yourself a simple question. "Do I want to be in this exact spot five years from now?"

If the answer is no, then start figuring out where you want to be in five years and in ten years. For those of you without any sense of business, this is called "Making a Business Plan."

—Be realistic in your planning. Do not set up failure, set up success.

For example, if you have never written three novels in one year, then don't have a business plan that has you creating three novels a year for five years. Remember, you can always change your business plan later when you actually produce three novels in a year.

Some people use my daily blogs as motivation. But don't try to match me from a dead stop. I have produced ten short novels in ten months while doing this blog. And about thirty short stories and parts of a bunch of other stuff on the fiction side, plus four nonfiction books. But I knew I could write a dozen short novels in a year, year after year, (my plan with my *Smith's Monthly* magazine) because I wrote eleven 90,000 word novels in one year once. And ten another year. I knew what it would take and I set my business plan for that.

—Figure in time to learn, to keep getting knowledge.

If you assume you will just "get better" in five years without study, wow are you delusional. Doesn't work that way in any art or any business.

Learning must be part of your business plan in both business and writing

skills, even if you get most of that from talking with other writers and reading blogs and buying a few books. Do something to focus on learning.

—Set a start date.

That is the most critical advice I can give you. After you have made a plan, set a start day to get going and then just get going.

—And keep going when life is nasty to you.

This is the real difference between short-term careers in writing and long-term careers. All of us old-timers who have been around for three or four or more decades have had life kick us to the ground a number of times. No writer gets through a decade without huge problems that stop everything cold.

When you get back on your feet and look around, you might feel behind. That's natural. Clear that, pick a start date, take a deep breath, and start again.

SUMMARY

The feeling of being behind, of missing a chance, hits all of us.

I am no exception. I had been going strong when my friend died three years ago and I lost a year to dealing with that estate. I somehow managed to stand up again, clear the feeling about the lost time, and reset a new business plan.

Those of you who have watched me writing in public the last ten months saw clearly that I had a few really bad months in the winter. I just kept plowing on through.

That's how this works.

"...there are two kinds of people in this world, those who wish and those who will, and the world and its goods will always belong to those who will."

So push aside the feeling of being behind, of feeling like you have missed out, set a business plan, and become a person who will...

Trust me, writing and publishing and having readers buy your books is a ton more fun than sitting around wishing.

And you all know how I like to have fun with my writing.

Sacred Cow #9
You Must Sell Your Books Cheaply to Make Any Money

THIS MYTH IS so nasty, it causes huge fights among indie writers. And the reason is that every indie writer believes they are right in their way of doing things in pricing. And yet wrong pricing, either too cheap or too expensive, can really hurt sales.

So what is the right answer? What is the right price?

That depends.

Some History

Back when electronic books came in, and when KDP opened up the gates to allow indie small press publishers in the door, electronic books were still a very new thing. Electronic books composed somewhere around a half of 1% of all books sold, if that.

But when those gates opened, authors, for the very first time had the complete freedom to value their own work to readers. And with that freedom came some very interesting decisions.

Authors had to balance value with discounts to get readers to buy in a new delivery form for fiction.

First off, a bunch of traditional published writers, me included, had a sense that electronic books had less value (we were used to paper so we could be forgiven that thinking early on). So when we started into selling electronic books, we priced our books at the lowest point allowed, which was 99 cents.

Joe Konrath, a traditionally published writer was the leader of this 99-cent movement.

But as time wore on in that first early stage, and it looked like ebooks were here to stay and were growing, many of us started realizing that we could price our books higher, but still lower than traditional publishers and make a ton of money and still give readers good deals. We didn't need to toss our books into the discount bin of 99 cents just to make a few sales.

In other words, readers were starting to value electronic books.

Traditional publishers helped indie publishers a lot in this very early period by deciding that they didn't like electronic books and priced them up near hardcover levels, as if an ebook was a specialty item.

And for a time, they postponed ebook releases for a year after the hardback as they used to do with mass market paperbacks.

After a year or so, I looked at both sides with head-shaking puzzlement. No way in hell was I going to get 35 cents for a sale of a novel (My share if I published a novel for 99 cents). I got a lot more per book in royalties than that from New York on a paperback sale.

But on the flip side, there was no way in hell was I going to price a novel in electronic form at $15.99.

Publishing needed a middle ground.

At this point, the traditional publishers got together to break the law and hold prices high and stop discounting. And indie publishers were still fighting among themselves about the right low price, racing to the bottom as I liked to call it.

After another year or so, what started to become clear as electronic books exploded in sales was that readers were buying electronic books in place of mass market paperbacks, the pocket-sized books that sold around $7.99. In fact, over the last few years, the mass market form of book continues to shrink in sales almost in direct relation to the growth in ebooks sales.

So it seemed to a lot of us that a logical place to price a novel was in the area just under the price of a mass market paperback. (The $4.99 to $7.99 price range.) That allowed authors to get the most value for their work and allowed readers to get a deal.

More WMG Writers' Guides
from all your favorite booksellers
in trade paper and electronic editions.

Eventually, the strident discount sellers in the indie world, including Joe Konrath, slowly brought their prices up. And the people running traditional publishing slowly brought some of their prices down into the $7.99 to $9.99 range for an electronic book.

So now, as I write this here in the middle of 2014, pricing on electronic books, in most cases, has stabilized in a range for novels.

That price range tends to be $2.99 to $9.99 for genre fiction novels, with the indie writers being on the $2.99 side (some at 99 cents still) and the traditional publishers being on the $9.99 side of the scale (some at $15.99 still).

The Danger of the Myth

To this day, you hear the indie writers shouting about pricing in the low ranges, saying everyone needs to do that. And that low range from 99 cents to $2.99 for a full novel has become known as a discount range.

But so many indie writers don't have a clue what the word "discount" even means.

And to make matters worse, new writers think, because they don't know business. They think their new novel has no value. What they don't realize is if they had sold their novel to a traditional publisher, it would have sold fine at the high price range.

So the beginning writers price their novel at the bottom of the scale out of sheer fear and being in a hurry to make as much as possible.

For them, that first bloom of sales often quickly vanishes, or in this new world of readers becoming aware, the sales don't happen much at all. And the new writer feels hopeless, stops writing, follows the myths of promotion, and lowers their price even more.

And eventually the new writer can see no reason to write the next book because they made so little money. Deadly.

Because of pricing and getting in a hurry, their dream is shattered.

What is Discounting?

I'm going to make this scary simple. Those of you who really understand publishing, don't laugh. I'm trying to make this plain and clear.

Discounting in the book industry comes in two forms.

The first form is the chains of stores called "discount stores" that take remainders from publishers, or buy cheap books published directly into the discount sales channels. (Book Warehouse is only one of a number of such bookstore chains. You usually find them in discount malls.)

The sale books you see up front in a B&N store are discount books, published for those shelves only, or high-discount books sold by the publisher for that table. (Authors make little or no money on high discount books sold like that.)

In this same area, there are the discount bins and tables that most indie bookstores have. Those are filled with books that didn't sell that the bookstore owner just wants out of the way. One indie owner here in our town has a cart that wheels out onto the front area of the store and it's full of ten-cent books.

The second form of discount is what are simply called sales. Amazon or GooglePlay always discounts books by some percent. That's one form of sale.

Or if you have your book priced at $5.99 and put it through BookBub for $2.99 for a short time, that's a discount.

And so on. Sales that lower a higher set price are called discounts.

The problem with starting your price of your book out so low in the first form, you have no room for the second part of discounting, and your main buyers are not necessarily loyal readers, but just discount buyers.

Pricing Your Book Because You Feel Insecure

Doing that is not a business strategy. That's a wake-up call that you need a confidence boost.

If you find yourself saying, "But I don't have a name so I should give my books away to get a name." You don't understand anything about this business.

And if you use the term, "I'm doing it to 'get readers,' you might want to really step back and look at your own reading habits.

Do you remember an author with one book that you stumbled upon and downloaded for free a year ago? And that author had nothing else at the time published. Do you honestly remember that author's name?

And if you downloaded it for free, did you even read it?

Building a fan base is one thing that is very real, and that comes over a lot of years and a lot of books. Put a newsletter sign-up on your website to see how many true fans you really have at the moment.

"Getting a reader" just doesn't work in any reality, especially when they didn't pay anything for the book.

Math For a Moment

Time to do a little math just for fun.

I am talking genre novels here. And I am only using Kindle pricing structure.

—Your Price...99 cents. You get 35 cents per sale.

—Your Price...$1.99. You get 70 cents per sale.

—Your Price...$2.99. You get $2.09 per sale.

—Your Price...$3.99. You get $2.79 per sale.

—Your Price...$4.99. You get $3.49 per sale.

—Your Price...$5.99. You get $4.19 per sale.

—Your Price...$6.99. You get $4.89 per sale.

—Your Price...$7.99. You get $5.59 per sale.

Now I am a business person. I know a lot of writers are not, but I am, so my concern is finding a right mix of sales vs. price to get the largest income.

And this is where the fun comes in for every indie publisher.

Most of us know that the 99 cent and $1.99 price for novels is just too low for anything but a short term sale of a novel.

But look at that $2.99 price. You need to ask yourself this: If you set your price at $2.99, would you sell twice as many copies as you would sell at $5.99 to make basically the same amount of money?

And would that sales rate sustain?

That's a decent business question and I honestly have no answer because, as I said above. It depends.

FOR ME PERSONALLY, I would like the $5.99 rate because it allows me to do sales along the way. I also like the $7.99 price because every sale makes a lot of nice income. And it looks better when discounted as well.

And I can bundle them, lowering the price per book down and still make great money.

And my books look close enough to traditional published prices as to not shout that they are not. I like having my books lumped in that area, just under the prices of traditional publishers. My books, in comparison, look like a deal compared to a $9.99 electronic book from Putnam.

But not a devalued deal.

But that's just me personally. As a business person, I like the upper three prices for the reasons I stated and a number more. But again, there are no right answers.

But if you don't look at that math when making the decision, chances are you are making a wrong decision for the wrong reasons.

This is a business. You have a product to sell. Each product is unique, so make the pricing decision on that, not on some myth belief that indie books must be priced low.

What About Short Fiction Pricing?

I personally price my short stories at $2.99 and then do a paper edition for the stand-alone story and price it at $4.99.

Do I expect many people to buy a short story in paper for $4.99? No, but I like them and am using them for other things, such as signed paper bundles and so on.

But the $4.99 price for a paper edition of the short story makes the $2.99 look better to the consumer and I do sell short stories at that price. Not a great deal, but some.

Would I sell more at 99 cents? Sure. Would I make more money with my short stories priced at 99 cents? Probably not.

For every story I sell, I get $2.09 cents at $2.99. I would get 35 cents at 99 cents. I would need six sales at 99 cents to make about the same amount as selling one at $2.99. I can't see that happening with short stories.

Plus, my stories are worth $2.99.

And to hold off a bunch of questions, that price is for anything under 10,000 words. Anything. I trust my readers to know if they want to have an experience for $2.99 or not. That's up to them.

Again, no right answer.

The freedom of indie publishing means you can set your own price for your own reasons.

But I suggest you look at real business reasons for each pricing choice.

Collections and Bundles?

I tend to price collections electronically around the same price as a novel, maybe a little less. (Right now I am in the process of redoing my few collections and doing a bunch more.) On bundles, it flat depends. No set answer at all.

USA TODAY BESTSELLING AUTHOR
DEAN WESLEY SMITH

HOW TO WRITE FICTION SALES COPY

WITH 32 COVERS AND EXAMPLES TO STUDY

A WMG WRITER'S GUIDE

More WMG Writers' Guides
from all your favorite booksellers
in trade paper and electronic editions.

Now interestingly enough, I do *Smith's Monthly*, an 80,000 word "collection" magazine every month with a full novel in it, four or five short stories, some nonfiction, and two serial novels.

I sell that electronically for less than what I sell the novel for when the novel comes out as a stand-alone a few months later. My fans are slowly picking up on that and subscribing to the *Monthly*, which gets them an even better deal.

That's my way.

Smith's Monthly is good value for content and price. My short stories are set where I am comfortable and they sell a few, my novels I set in the price range just under traditional, but not much.

Those are my business choices. And what is great fun, I get to make the choices.

And so do you.

Genre Does Matter

No discussion of pricing in this moment in time would be even close to complete without mentioning genre.

Electronic books are major factors now in many genres, even though across all of publishing electronic books are around the 23% level of all book sales. But in some genres, that number has soared past 50% and is still climbing. And in erotica, it might be approaching 100% for all I know.

So with your pricing business decisions, you must be aware of your genre. For example, many, many readers in romance are near discount readers. They are rabid readers who can devour three or four books per day without an issue. So price is critical to them.

And romance writers have always been fast writers, but now even they have had to pick up speed to keep their readers

satisfied. So if you are writing into the romance or erotica genres, you would be better served to price down in the $2.99 to $3.99 area.

On the other side of the coin, mystery and thriller readers are paper readers, and high value readers. Electronic sales are not large yet in the mystery genre.

Mystery readers will spend $8.99 for a mass market paperback or $27.99 for a hardback. There are very, very few discount mystery readers, so you would be better served to shout to the mystery readers that your books have value electronically and get the price in the $6.99 to $7.99 range. And make sure you have a paper edition as well.

Genre plays into your business decisions on pricing. Never forget that.

SUMMARY

Pricing for indie publishers has settled into a range from $2.99 to $7.99 for electronic novels. Depending on a host of factors.

Every publisher, every author, needs to decide for themselves how they want to present themselves to readers.

Every publisher needs to understand the reality of their own genre.

So my suggestions to you to help you find your right price for a book:

1...Look at your genre and the pricing of the other books in that genre. Both traditional and indie.

2...Start your book slightly higher than you feel is right. You can do sales to give readers deals.

3...Take a long approach. Put your book up at a price and go back to writing. Check the income and sales per month, but don't touch the price (except for a special sale like a BookBub) for one year.

(See Chapter Six on Giving Your Garden Time to Grow.)

4...When you have four or five books in a series, but not before, think about discounting the first one down some (but not too low) to draw in readers. And do sales and special promotions on that first book to get readers into the series. That's the time you can start using price as a really effective weapon in sales.

5...Watch what the traditional publishers are doing for electronic books in your genre at least once per year and stay just below them. That will make your book look professional, yet give readers a deal. Again, a long-term effective way to use the power of price.

6...Get a long-term business plan and stick with it. And by long term, I mean at least five years or more. At least. And most of that plan should be focused on writing, not pricing.

Every indie publisher now has the choice of what to price their own books. Every indie publisher is different.

More WMG Writers' Guides
from all your favorite booksellers
in trade paper and electronic editions.

Base your pricing decisions on a business plan, set the price on a book, and forget it for a year before looking at the price decision again. (Except for sales.)

This choice is a wonderful thing we now all have.

But don't let the choice drive you away from your writing.

Set it, forget it.

Go have fun writing the next book.

Sacred Cow #10
There Is Only One Way to Publish a Book

THIS MYTH IS so flat wrong, it's funny. Yet you hear writers arguing and getting angry at other writers because the other writer is not doing something "right," as if there is a "right" or "wrong" way.

Nope.

The right way is your way, the way that makes you happy, makes you money.

Some History

Almost from the beginning of indie publishing, bloggers, me included, were giving our opinions of this new world. And we all gave suggestions with our opinions. Joe Konrath, Barry Eisler, Kristine Kathryn Rusch, and I all are from traditional publishing and our opinions, good or bad, at first were colored by our experiences living for decades in that traditional system.

Some of what we suggested was right, some got dated quickly. I still think the best book written on this freelance lifestyle for indie writers was by Kris called *The Freelancer's Survival Guide.*

And what Joe and Barry have done over the years to keep all of us headed in decent directions has been stunning. And now Hugh Howey and Data Guy, along with The Passive Guy, are flowing information to all of us so fast, it's sometimes hard to keep up.

As this publishing world has expanded for writers, so have the options and the ways of making great money in this publishing business.

In traditional publishing, the road was set for you. Write a lot and get better and submit until you got an agent who then could help you sell books.

When I came in ahead of the agent-control phase, the path was write a lot, meet editors at conferences, sell your books to them, have your agent fetch the coffee and chase the money.

That was the path. Simple and clear.

Now the path is not simple and it is far, far from clear.

And anyone who tells you there is only one way to do something now in publishing just hasn't got their head up out of the sand. Or they just time-traveled from the last century forward.

Some Options

Option #1...Do Everything Yourself.

This option is how many of us started working on the indie side, and many still do. The writer does everything himself, from covers to blurbs to trading with friends for proofing. The writer puts the books on the bookstore sites, promotes what they can, and goes back to writing.

What is nice about this method to start is the learning curve is steep, yes, but it is possible. And all the money is yours that comes in.

There is very, very little real set costs with this method. Some art, maybe a business license, that's it. The time to write the book is the biggest overall cost.

I tend to suggest all writers start this way with their indie publishing business because it teaches you many things about the publishing business.

Option #2...Hire Some Stuff Done.

This option works well for those who don't feel they can do their own covers, or who don't want to tackle the chore of doing epubs and getting things launched on different sites.

At a certain point, almost all writers hire at least a good copyeditor. That's critical.

This option, in theory, gives you more time to write, but in the long run, really doesn't. You are spending time making sure things are done, often more time than if you learned how to do the task yourself.

Another downside on this option is the upfront costs. This limits your ability to write a lot of things like I am doing.

The good side is you don't have the learning curve of knowing what makes a great cover. The bad side is that you don't have that learning curve as to know what makes a great cover, so your sales are dependent on someone else's ideas of a good cover. That is always dangerous.

Option #3...You Only Write, and Hire Everything Else.

This option is used by many, many traditional writers who are working to get their backlist up and write new books at the same time.

This option is done in two ways.

One way is to hire a company like Lucky Bat Books and see if they will take and do your book for you. They do the copyediting, professional covers, lay everything out, and set up the accounts for you. All for a fee and you get all the money.

This option is great for a slower writer who only does a book a year or so. Retired age writers do this a great deal and it's a great choice.

The other way is the way Kris and I did it. I started off (after my traditional years) in Option #1, letting the money build up, then we slowly started hiring help as the money increased, and now, except for my magazine, *Smith's Monthly*, we have full-time employees building a business that publishes our books and stories, among other projects.

Option #4...Sell Your Book to a Small Press.

This has some good and bad points to it, and everything depends on the contract you sign. If they can't pay you anything up front, caution. They may be offering a good royalty split, but chances are you might not see your half of the split if the owner of the small press needs to pay a house payment that month.

Small presses always depend on who is in charge. Watch your contract, be able to get out quick.

But the nice thing is that they do the work for you at their cost. The bad thing is that they might put a really ugly cover on your book and keep your money.

It's an option, but caution, some of the great horror stories come from writers who went to small presses.

Option #5...Sell Your Book to Traditional Publishing.

This is a very long and slow process now, with a lot of issues with it. It might take four or five years to get your book into print, and that's if it fits some

unknown publishing vision of an editor and you are lucky.

From agents to bad contracts to bad editing, traditional publishing isn't a path I would suggest until things level out.

Many traditional companies are going to be in financial hurt and shutting down entire imprints and merging and laying off editors over the next few years. It's a mine field you would have to be scary lucky to make it through.

Remember, I published over 100 books with traditional publishers and this new world of traditional publishing flat scares me. I'd rather go play poker again than sell a book back into that mess. But that's just my opinion. Make your own decision.

Option #6...Have Your Agent Publish Your Books for You.

This again is full of all sorts of issues, including money issues. Your agent has suddenly become a publisher and is collecting money on your sales, money you can't account for because your agent gets it all first, and then takes a cut and sends you the rest. You can only hope it's the right amount.

Plus agents have fifty clients they are doing this for, so your book will get no attention. And chances are they are hiring out most jobs as well. I don't see this option being around for more than another ten years max as agencies collapse under the weight and lack of money. They will take your money with them when they go down. That is a proven fact in just the last year.

Option #7...Brand New Forms of Publishing Businesses.

This is part of the fun of this new world. I've seen numbers of new forms of publishing starting up. Authors grouping together to share skills, forming a co-op of sorts. Authors grouping together to form publishing companies like Kris and I have done to get more clout in promotion and sales and distribution.

The key with this path is be careful and watch who has control of the money.

Option #8, 9, and so on...Who knows what will be invented or is blooming right now for options for writers.

So many new things are coming along, the best thing we can all do is keep our eyes open and be willing to take a look at a new option when it opens up. It's a wonderful new world.

Caution on the scam publishers out there.

Every traditional publishing company now has a pay-to-play publishing imprint or two or three imprints, that are similar to the old vanity press scams of ten years ago. I don't consider those an option and I hope no one reading this does either.

The Harm of this Myth

The sad thing about this myth of believing there is only one way is that it doesn't just apply to indie publishers, but to all writers. In fact, this myth is chanted the loudest to the young writers coming in that think that there is only one way: Get an agent, sell a book.

Get an agent, sell a book.

Get an agent, sell a book.

Get an agent, sell a book.

It's like a bad nightmare.

Nope, it is far from the only way to get your book to readers who will love it.

Another area of harm is when this myth invades a writer's writing mind.

The writer starts thinking that the only way to make it is have fifty books and the writer must write a dozen books a year and work a day job and have family time with kids.

Well, gang, you watch me write a novel a month on my Writing in Public blog, but remember, I've been doing this for almost forty years. And I write short novels, seldom over 50,000 words long. And I live with another writer and we have no children.

In my first few years of writing seriously, I was excited I managed a short story per week. If I had been able to watch a Silverberg or a Resnick writing at my pace now (They did, and faster), I would have been stunned that it was even possible, and if I had tried it back then, I would have been frustrated and just quit. That's the truth.

So don't let anyone tell you there is only one way to produce words. There is your way. I would suggest that if you are writing a certain way and only producing one novel every year, you may want to explore other ways until you find something that helps you pick up speed.

But if you don't want to pick up speed, then don't. No right way, only your way.

You Must Write (blank)
to Make a Living

Holy crap, any time you hear anyone say that, just laugh in his or her face. Or let me know and I'll laugh at them.

That is flat the dumbest advice and the most harmful advice anyone could ever give.

And if you hear yourself thinking that you should move to (blank) genre to make more sales, laugh at yourself.

Folks, the best way to get to riches with your writing is flat be an artist. Protect your work, write what makes you passionate, what you love, what makes you angry, or as Stephen King says, what scares you.

Write to passion.

Never write to market.

Who knows, maybe what you are writing will be the next hot things and you will look like a genius for being out ahead of all the followers.

SUMMARY

In this modern world of publishing, there is no one way, no right way, no perfect path.

My suggestion is to keep your eyes open on the publishing side, look around, try one way or another, and be willing to change if something sounds right.

Do a writing plan and a business plan as to where you want to be in five years and figure out if the plan is realistic for your writing.

Write to passion.

And never listen to anyone who tells you there is only one right way.

There is only your way.

Experiment, learn, find it, and have fun.

USA Today Bestselling Writer

DEAN WESLEY SMITH

NOT EASY TO KILL THE LIGHT NEXT DOOR

A Bryant Street Story

Very strange things happen on Bryant Street.

For Cayden Cavanaugh, getting rid of a light to guard the neighborhood became his passion.

He thought of nothing else.

A simple story of a light and a man with passion. But on Bryant Street, nothing remains simple for long.

NOT EASY TO KILL
THE LIGHT NEXT DOOR
A Bryant Street Story

CAYDEN CAVANAUGH WAS done.

Fed up.

Last straw.

Over his limit.

And every other damn cliché a person could think of.

The light had to go.

And he would make it go. That stupid white light towering over Bob and Stephie's garage had cost him sleep, his job, his wife, and most of his money. In a few days it would cost him this house.

The light would pay.

And it would pay tonight.

He should have done this long ago.

Cayden sat at the table in his once beautiful and modern suburban kitchen. His former wife Hanna had insisted on the best white granite counters, the most expensive light-blue glass-tile backsplash, and top range steel appliances when they built this dream home. He had loved every bit of it.

Now he could only see those things by the light mounted above the garage next door. He had no money to pay the power bill and the power had been turned off three days ago.

But Cayden could see enough from the light next door to load the pistol he had bought two days before.

Tonight the light would pay.

The sink was full of unwashed dishes and they smelled like rotten fish, but Cayden no longer cared. Hanna was long gone and he would be soon. He couldn't hold off the bank any longer. They were taking the dream home, taking everything, and all because of that stupid light.

And even leaving the house, moving to another city, another country, he knew he would never escape that light. He had to finish this once and for all right now, tonight.

Things had been fine just a short year before.

Then at one summer neighborhood barbeque Bob had told him he was putting in a security light on his garage, on a pole sticking up from the garage peak. Bob said it would cost a bunch, but it would make his house safer and also the entire area.

Cayden had thought it a wonderful idea.

How stupid had he been?

So three weeks later, when the light first clicked on as the sun set, Cayden was stunned at how bright it was. So bright that it seemed to fill every room in Cayden and Hanna's house with a dull white light that washed out all the colors they had so carefully picked.

He and Hanna took to closing the blinds at night, but for Cayden the light still seemed to fill everything. It felt like a disease eating away at something that had once been beautiful.

Hanna said she didn't much notice the light with the blinds pulled, but Cayden hated it with a passion. As far as he was concerned, the light was ruining everything they had built.

A month later they put up those room-darkening blinds for their bedroom and the rooms on the side of the house facing Bob and Stephie's home. At that point Cayden was having trouble sleeping and getting more and more angry at the slightest things.

But most especially at all the light and how it washed everything out.

The darkening shades didn't seem to help, even though Hanna said the room was pitch black.

It wasn't pitch black.

The light was there.

Cayden could see it.

He could feel it.

It kept him awake.

He knew it attacked the walls of his home like a tiny army never letting up. It was always right outside the window, right against the walls, flooding the roof, trying to get in at the slightest mistake on his part.

He wasn't sure why Hanna couldn't see the gray in how the light out there was so strong it took even total blackness and robbed it of power.

Two months after the light first came on, Cayden went to Bob and asked him to take it down. Cayden said he would even pay for the cost of the light.

Bob said it made him and Stephie feel safer, so he refused.

A month later Cayden and Bob got into a fight over the light and Cayden slugged Bob. Actually it seems that he did more than just slug him, although

Cayden didn't remember most of it he was so angry. Turns out he put Bob in the hospital and Bob pressed charges.

Cayden spent two nights in jail and still had his case pending for trial.

Then Cayden found himself yelling more and more at Hanna and finally three months ago she left to go live with her parents. She begged him to get professional help.

He knew he was fine.

It was all the light's fault.

The light was eating at him.

At work, about the time Hanna left, Cayden noticed the light had followed him to work, that it was washing out all the colors in his office. He started working with the lights off and the blinds pulled to try to block out the light, but it still got in.

He got angrier and angrier.

The light had now infected everything.

A week later he lost his job.

His boss told him to get help.

Cayden knew he was fine. He didn't know why everyone kept telling him to get help, that he wasn't his old self. He knew he would be fine as soon as he got rid of the light.

Tonight he would do just that.

Finally.

Cayden looked around at the dark kitchen, a room that had many good memories. He was going to miss this home as much as he missed Hanna.

Then he made sure the gun was loaded and stood. It was time to face the devil.

Once he had won, maybe he and Hanna could start over, plan a new life in a new home, away from the light.

Maybe get some color back in their lives.

Holding the now loaded pistol in his right hand, he went out the back door into the yard that seemed so bright it could be daylight. The gun felt extra heavy, far heavier than it had felt in the store when he bought it.

That evil light above Bob and Stephie's garage seemed to flood his entire yard, washing out the wonderful shades of darkness with a pale, white world of blandness.

His barbeque no longer looked black, but a light gray. The green grass looked almost pink. The dark, oak-stained fence seemed like it had been painted dull white.

The light was so powerful it leached all the color out of everything, just as it had leached away his life.

He turned toward the fence to get closer to the light and then realized it felt like he was walking upstream against rushing water.

The light knew what he was planning and wanted to stop him.

He would not stop.

He had to win this fight.

He leaned into the light, focusing on the sidewalk in front of him with every step, the gun in his hand getting heavier and heavier.

Now it felt like he was in a strong wind that seemed to get stronger and stronger with each step.

And the light got brighter, if that was possible.

He finally stopped and planted both feet firmly. Then he looked up at the light.

It blinded him like looking into the sun.

The pain was intense, filling his entire head.

He wanted to scream in agony, but somehow he managed to raise the pistol and fire at the white light above him.

The sound was so loud it shocked him. It echoed over the neighborhood and a dog barked.

He staggered back, the pain in his head worse.

The light still blinded him.

He couldn't let it win that easily.

He fired at it again.

And then again.

He heard glass shattering, but the light was still as bright, if not brighter.

He fired over and over until finally the gun clicked empty and he dropped it.

He then sat down, his back to the light, shaking.

The light had won.

Everything around him was still washed out of all color and his eyes burnt from looking into the brightness.

The pain in his head radiated out like someone was poking sharp sticks into his eyes.

He finally just lay down, staring upward into the white light. He was in too much pain and too tired to move.

The light had won.

He was not sure how long it was until the police arrived and led him to the police car.

He could barely see any of it because of the bright light and the stabbing pain in his head.

By the time he reached the station he could only see white, with wonderful blackness around the edges.

A short time later he found himself in the hospital with a police guard. A young-sounding doctor was trying to shine a light into his eyes.

But Cayden couldn't see the light.

Or the doctor for that matter.

The blackness had slowly crept in from the sides of his vision until finally, thankfully, everything was black.

Everything.

The light was gone.

He had finally killed it.

He could finally sleep.

The next thing he heard was Hanna talking with a doctor. They were talking about him and an operation it seemed he had had.

Around him machines beeped and there were sounds of others talking out in the hallway.

The intense pain in his head was gone replaced by a dull ache and everything was blissfully black.

It felt wonderful to hear Hanna's voice again. Calming, not at all like the last time he had talked with her. He couldn't remember now why he had been so angry.

"We got the tumor completely," the doctor told Hanna. "But we don't think his vision will ever return I'm afraid. Just too much damage."

Cayden wanted to smile, to shout for joy, but instead he just lay there, not moving.

Blackness was fine by him.

The blackness was a victory.

He had fought the light and he had won and that was all that mattered.

He never wanted to see light again.

In blackness maybe he could live again.

More Bryant Street Stories
Available at your favorite booksellers.

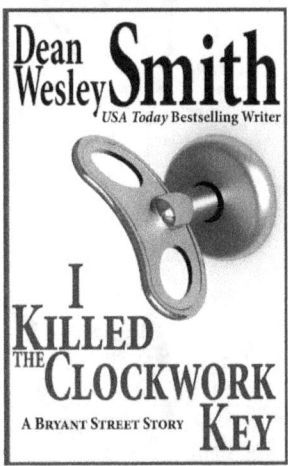

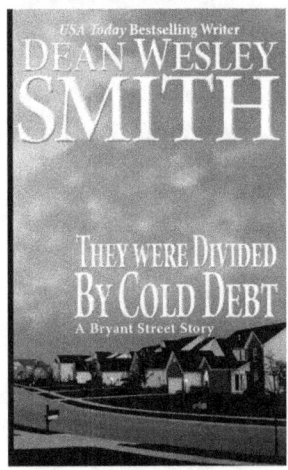

USA *Today* Bestselling Writer

DEAN WESLEY SMITH

AN IMMORTALITY OF SORTS

A Buckey The Space Pirate Story

Buckey the Space Pirate's mother just died.

Fred, his talking oak tree best friend, loved reciting limericks more than anything. But not this day.

Instead of limericks, Fred gives Buckey and his wife Mary something far more special as a gift.

He gives them a true understanding of the meaning of time travel.

A heartwarming Buckey story without one lewd limerick. Go figure.

AN IMMORTALITY OF SORTS
A Buckey the Space Pirate Story

"I AM VERY sorry for the loss of your mother," Fred said, his voice seeming to come from everywhere around the young oak tree in my mother's back yard.

The early spring day had turned out nice, just warm enough that I didn't need a jacket. The yard was still in winter growth, but I was starting to see some small shoots of green coming up. The twenty-foot oak tree showed no signs of any leaves budding yet. It wouldn't be long until they did and the lawn needed to be mowed.

Fred was my best friend outside of Mary, my wife, who Fred had introduced me to. Fred was a talking oak tree that could travel through all history into all other oak trees. He could take me and Mary with him as well, which was how I met her.

She was a widow who had lived in a small log cabin in the late 1800s outside of Boise, Idaho, surrounded by oak trees.

I was from modern times, a kid who in college used to dress up like a space pirate to impress girls at parties and science fiction conventions. That was how I got my name Buckey.

Now Mary and I were both twenty-seven and living in a brand new home we had built on her property that we had arranged in the past to come down through time for me to inherit here in my present.

Yes, I didn't exist in Mary's time and she was already dead in my time, yet we were happily married. Time travel with oak trees could sometimes get very confusing.

I always kept an acorn in my pocket and Mary always kept two acorns, one on a gold chain around her neck, another in her pocket. As long as we had an acorn from an oak tree, or were over an oak tree's roots, we remained in each other's time.

In other words, with an acorn in my pocket, I could go anywhere in her time and if she wore the acorn here, she could go anywhere in this time.

Mostly we spent our time here, in our new modern home built where her old log cabin used to stand in her time.

But Fred, the young talking oak tree I had rescued seven years before, was planted in my mother's back yard. I had nowhere else to plant it at the time.

And just three days ago we had buried my mother. She had died far too young after a short fight against cancer.

Luckily, she had lived long enough to see Mary and me get married. I had never seen her so happy. She had loved Mary like the daughter she never had.

My mother had been well-liked and the large church we used for her funeral was jammed with her friends coming to pay their last respects. She had worked most of her life as an RN, and she had loved it, working right up to a few weeks before the cancer took her.

I could not believe my mother was gone.

Mary was inside and we were just starting to clean out some of my mother's things. We had no intention of selling the house, because this back yard was where Fred lived. Mom had left me the house, since I was her only child and dad had died when I was five.

But she had wanted much of her stuff to go to different charities and Mary and I had promised her we would take care of it. But I could only stand so much, so I had gone out to sit and talk with Fred.

"Thank you," I said to Fred as I dropped into one of the lawn chairs near him and facing away from my mother's house. Three years ago I had fenced in the back yard with a tall fence and dozens more small oak trees growing along the fence so the neighbors couldn't see me sitting out here talking to the air.

Mary and I had often sat and talked with Fred, even though we could talk to him anywhere there was an oak tree, or if we were carrying the acorns.

But there was something special about just sitting with Fred, the twenty-foot oak tree, knowing he was the real Fred.

And Fred seemed to enjoy our company in person as well.

After I sat there in silence for a time, just not really thinking, trying to get the image of the funeral and all the work ahead to take care of Mom's things out of my head, Fred finally spoke.

"Your mother was a very amazing woman."

I nodded. "She was."

Then Fred said something that damn near knocked me over backwards out of my lawn chair.

"I enjoyed our conversations and travels."

I stood up, staring at the bare branches of the young oak tree in front of me.

"You talked to my mother?"

"Of course," Fred said. "Long before you were born, actually. Your father was an amazing man as well."

"You talked to my dad?"

"Of course," Fred said. "I helped introduce the two of them."

My head was spinning and I had no idea what to think.

I turned to the house and in my loudest voice shouted, "Mary!"

A moment later Mary came out the back door, looking slightly panicked.

Every day I thought of her as the most beautiful woman in the world in any time. She was five-five with long brown hair and the largest brown eyes of any woman I had ever met.

And those eyes could see right through a person.

And right now I really needed her to help me get a grip on the reality I felt slipping away.

"You all right?" she asked as she came quickly off the back porch and down to where I was standing.

"Fred says he talked with my parents."

"Of course I did," Fred said, his voice rumbling through the yard and off the tall wooden fence.

If a young oak tree could sound indignant, Fred did at that moment.

"I have always told you that you two are not the only two humans I talk with through time."

"Wow, that is wonderful," Mary said.

She clearly wasn't as shocked at the news as I was. I always considered my mother a rock-of-the-earth person, not someone who talked to time-traveling oak trees.

"I also talked with your parents, Mary," Fred said.

At that Mary leaned against me and I thought her legs were going to go out.

I got her seated in one of the lawn chairs and then I took the other before my legs gave way as well.

I sat there, holding her hand as we had done so often over the last few years in these chairs, staring up into the bare branches of the small tree.

"How come you didn't tell us?" I asked.

Fred chuckled. "As I have said many times before in different situations, you did not ask. The greatest human failing is the inability to ask the right question at the right time."

The oak tree then chuckled and again the sound seemed to echo through the spring day and around the enclosed back yard.

"Besides," Fred said, "your mother asked me not to say anything until she died and I would never go against your mother's wishes, you know. She was a smart, formidable, and very strong human. And besides, she liked my limericks."

I nodded to that. She had been strong, but not once had I ever heard her repeat a limerick. Especially one of Fred's limericks. They were often quite racy, to say the least.

It seemed that Fred got bored standing all the time in one spot and to amuse himself through the centuries, he made up limericks. In the last few years I had had printed two of his books of limericks. They were selling fairly well, actually, which made Fred want to come up with even more.

"What were my parents like?" Mary asked, her voice soft and low.

I knew she had never really got a chance to know them. They were both killed in a train wreck outside of Chicago when Mary was ten and Mary had been raised by an aunt and uncle who brought her west to Idaho.

"They were very much like you," Fred said. "Smart, kind, loving."

Mary nodded. "Would you tell me how you started talking with them?"

"It will be my pleasure," Fred said.

Then for the next ten minutes he relayed the story of how he first started talking with Mary's mother, then her father.

Fred chuckled. "They both, to the day they sadly died, believed they were slightly daft, as your mother put it."

Mary smiled at that.

"Would you tell me how you started to talk with my parents?" I asked.

"I met your father first outside of Boston just after the Revolutionary War," Fred said.

If Mary hadn't been holding onto my hand, I would have gone over backwards in the lawn chair.

"Buckey's father was from the past?" Mary asked because I was just sitting there trying to not pass out.

"He was," Fred said. "A dashing man who fought and was injured in the Revolutionary War. He was a landowner and farmer by trade. There were many oak trees on his property and as he recovered from his wounds from the war, sitting in the shade of a giant oak tree, we started talking."

"Are those wounds what eventually killed him?" I asked.

My mother had said something along those lines, but would never elaborate.

"To my understanding, yes," Fred said. "He would have died that first summer, but I asked your mother for help and took her to him. I told them about the acorns and she got him into a modern hospital and they saved his life."

"My mother saved my father's life after the Revolutionary War?" I asked.

"She did," Fred said.

At that point the yard was spinning and if not for the solidness of Mary's hand, I am certain I would have just slid down to lie on the grass.

"They were married six months later," Fred said. "In a wonderful ceremony on his land during his time. Then they also married in this time in a small ceremony. Both ceremonies were beautiful, both outdoors under large oak trees."

I was still so stunned I flat didn't know what to say.

After a moment, my wonderful wife said, "Would it be possible for us to watch my parents' wedding and then Buckey's parents' two weddings?"

"Of course," Fred said.

And for the next hour we watched three weddings, two very historical and one in a small chapel here and now. We stood in the back, like ghosts, unable to be seen.

I agreed with Fred, all three were wonderful.

And when we returned to my mother's back yard, the grief of losing my mother had lifted.

Mary seemed lighter and was smiling as well.

"Thank you," Mary said. "That was wonderful."

"Yes, thank you," I said.

"It is always my pleasure," Fred said.

I needed to clear up one thing. "Fred, may I ask a question?"

"Of course," he said.

I was sure that if an oak tree could smile a satisfied smile, Fred would be doing so.

"My mother, my father, Mary's parents. They are not really dead, are they?"

The twenty-foot oak tree just chuckled. "The right question at the right time. You are learning. To answer your question, they do not exist in this time and place."

"But they are still alive in their own times and their own places?" I asked. "Is that correct?"

Mary squeezed my hand, clearly understanding where I was going.

"That is correct," Fred said.

"So tomorrow evening, if we threw a dinner party for our parents, all four of them," I said, "they could attend?"

"Of course," Fred said.

I glanced at Mary and she was beaming. "I am dead in this time," she said. "Yet I am here."

I was finally starting to understand.

"So over the years since my father died," I asked, "has my mother spent time with him?"

"Yes," Fred said, "if you insist on thinking in linear time. Your mother and father existed for their life spans, but that does not mean they do not still exist in many other times and places."

"Thanks to you," I said.

"I am not the only oak tree who tries to help humans understand their own abilities in time."

I started to open my mouth to ask what he meant, but Mary squeezed my hand. That would be a conversation, a question for another time, another place.

"Fred," Mary said, "would you ask our parents to join us for dinner tomorrow evening?"

"I would be honored," Fred said. "But don't you think it would be nicer to invite them yourself?"

At that, the back door to my mother's house opened and my mother and father walked out, hand-in-hand, followed by another couple dressed in clothing from the 1800s.

All four of them were smiling as they came down off the porch toward us.

"Mom? Dad?" Mary whispered as she stood.

I tried to stand and turn, but failed, and finally did go over backwards in the lawn chair.

But somehow, with Fred and all four parents laughing, with Mary's help, I managed to scramble to my feet just in time to say hello and hug my dead parents as Mary hugged hers.

Behind me, I heard the young oak tree sigh a happy sigh.

~

  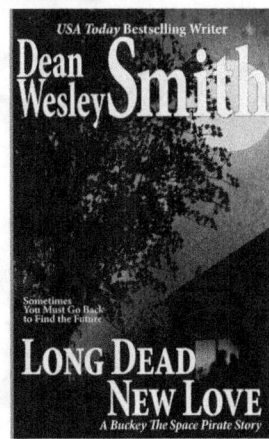

USA TODAY BESTSELLING AUTHOR

DEAN WESLEY SMITH

TOMBSTONE CANYON

A THUNDER MOUNTAIN NOVEL

Tombstone Dan loved his life in the Old West. He loved building a wonderful home in a hidden canyon.

Over a hundred years later, known as one of the best forensic historians in the business, Margaret "Maggie" Lund finds herself faced with the impossible task of discovering if Tombstone Dan really existed.

Two lives a hundred years apart twisting through history together.

Written with attention to the real details of the Old West, Tombstone Canyon adds another riveting tale into the Thunder Mountain series of adventures.

TOMBSTONE CANYON
A Thunder Mountain Novel

PART ONE
A New Home

PROLOGUE

August 17th, 2018
Boise, Idaho

"You ever hear of a man by the name of Tombstone Dan?" Dawn Edwards asked Duster Kendal.

The question sort of echoed around the big underground rock cavern under the Institute for Historical Research. The flat floor of the cavern was full of dozens of comfortable couches and chair groupings, a large number in front of a large stone fireplace against one wall. Everything was cloth and in brown tones, including the area rugs under some of the chairs and coffee tables.

Three were numbers of reading lights and fake plants around each sitting area, trying to give it a feeling of home. It was designed to be about as comfortable for a lot of people as a large, high-ceilinged rock cavern could be.

Right now the cavern smelled of chicken soup and fresh bread, a combination that made Dawn instantly hungry.

The cavern had been designed so that numbers of group conversations could go on at the same time and was often called the "living room" of the complex. It most certainly worked as the center of the place and Dawn always felt at home when she entered the big room.

Duster and Bonnie Kendal sat at a large kitchen counter that ran for almost twenty paces along one wall. The counter had enough stools that it could sit two-dozen people, although Dawn had never seen more than five or six ever sitting at that massive thing.

On the other side of the counter, built into one rock wall, was a full kitchen with a number of stoves and three different fridges and freezers stretched along the length. The cavern could hold a hundred people comfortably and the kitchen was designed to serve that many with just as much ease. It had all been designed to last for hundreds of years in the future. And every few years the appliances and furniture were updated.

Right now only about twenty-six people in the entire world even knew of the cavern or that the entire underground complex even existed in the center of Boise, Idaho. The Institute added a few researchers and scientists every year, but not near enough to fill this large space for a century or more.

"Colorful name," Duster said, shaking his head at Dawn's question about Tombstone Dan.

Usually Duster wore a long, dark brown oilcloth coat and a cowboy hat and in many timelines in the Old West he was known as Marshal Duster Kendal. But this afternoon in the cavern living area, he only wore jeans, cowboy boots, and a modern dress shirt with the sleeves rolled up.

He was sipping on a bowl of chicken soup and had a partially finished turkey sandwich on a plate beside his soup.

Beside him, Bonnie, his wife, had her long brown hair down and had on a tan silk blouse and jeans and tennis shoes. She had a finished bowl of soup in front of her.

The two looked perfectly normal, even though they were the two smartest minds on the planet, especially in mathematics. Because of discovering how to jump to other timelines, they both had lived for more thousands of years than Dawn wanted to think about.

Dawn had actually been alive for more thousands of years now than she wanted to think about. After the first thousand she had given up counting.

Even as long as they'd lived, all of them looked like they were in their early thirties.

Dawn had on a blue silk blouse and jeans and tennis shoes and had her long hair tied back. She and her husband Madison had been the first two historical researchers Bonnie and Duster had ever allowed to go back in time in another timeline. Since then the four of them had built the Historical Institute and pretty much ran things, even though Director Parks actually ran the day-to-day happenings of the Institute.

Bonnie also shook her head at the question about knowing a Tombstone Dan and went to working on her ham sandwich.

Dawn went around to the fridge and got a bottle of water. She had just come in from the Institute's main library in downtown Boise and the August sun had been warm. The comfortable and consistently slightly cool temperature of the cavern felt wonderful.

This entire crazy research on this one name had her going nuts. She had spent hundreds of years in different timelines living in Roosevelt, Idaho during the nine years it was alive, doing research on a number of books. She was considered the expert on the town that had existed and was now under a lake. She thought she knew everything about that small mining boomtown there was to know.

It seems she was wrong.

"Soup still on the stove," Bonnie said.

"Too hot," Dawn said, laughing. "You two do know it's August out there."

"Soup is good anytime of the year," Duster said.

Bonnie pointed at him and nodded her agreement.

Dawn went back to the fridge and got out some cold ham and a bottle of Dijon mustard. Then got two wonderful-smelling pieces of fresh bread from an open loaf on the counter and started to make herself a sandwich.

"So who is this Tombstone Dan guy?" Duster asked as he finished his soup and went back to working on his sandwich.

"Supposedly," Dawn said, looking around at Bonnie and Duster, "he owned all six of the major saloons in Roosevelt along Main Street."

Both Bonnie and Duster's heads snapped up to look at her.

Dawn laughed. Both of them had looks of total shock and disbelief on their faces.

Just as she had done, they also had lived many, many times in that old mining town of Roosevelt, Idaho. And in 1902, the four of them had built the huge Monumental Lodge above the town of Roosevelt.

Nothing should have surprised any of them about the mining town of Roosevelt and that entire Monumental Valley. And that's what was driving Dawn crazy. A very, very hidden bank record showed that a man going by the name of Tombstone Dan owned all the saloons.

"From what little I can find, he might have been a professional gambler, poker only," Dawn said, "who came to Roosevelt right at the start of the town, built the different saloons, brought in the pianos, and spent his nights all summer playing poker supposedly to help support his saloons. But that last part is just me making a bad guess. I honestly have no idea. None."

"Got a picture of this guy?" Duster asked.

Dawn shook her head. "Nothing. He appeared in some Roosevelt records and vanished when the town went under water."

"Do you have any information at all about him?" Bonnie asked.

"Nothing at all past what I just told you," Dawn said. "That's what is driving me so crazy."

"I could have sworn that those saloons were owned by three different men and a consortium out of Boise," Duster said.

"That is what we were supposed to believe," Dawn said, "but the evidence I have is pretty conclusive. He was behind the consortium and owned and built all six of the major saloons. The three men we know about just ran the places."

"What were the poker games like in them?" Bonnie asked Duster.

Dawn wanted to ask him the same thing, now. In her historical books about the town, she hadn't dealt at all with any-thing that went on in the saloons. Her interests had been in the people who lived in that harsh valley and survived and sometimes made a living out of what they did.

"Standard early 1900s poker games," Duster said, the remainder of his sand-wich now forgotten. "No one stood out as a professional besides Pete from California in the summer of 1904, but he only stayed a few months and left."

"So how did this owner of the saloons get the nickname Tombstone Dan?" Bonnie asked. "Any information about that?"

"I'm not so sure if that was a nick-name," Dawn said. "I found legal doc-uments in two Boise bank records with that name as a signature."

"Okay, now that is really, really weird," Duster said. "Sure he's not one of us from a future time?"

Dawn shook her head. "I checked with Director Parks and no one by that name is a researcher that hasn't started on board yet. Or is a researcher who will start in the next hundred years, at least that we know of. But since we don't have a picture and a real name, Director Parks can't be sure."

"Really odd," Bonnie said.

"Driving me crazy for the last month," Dawn said. "So if you two don't mind, I'm bringing in some help on the research. The woman I'm thinking of might end up being a candidate for the cavern here."

"That good, huh?" Bonnie asked, standing and picking up her bowl and empty sandwich plate and carrying it around the end of the bar toward the dishwasher.

"Professor Margaret Lund from the University of Wisconsin," Dawn said.

"She has been on our list," Bonnie said.

The four of them always had a list going of major researchers from around the world who could benefit from what the Institute did. Most of the time they invited the researchers to just come and research, all expenses paid, without ever knowing about the caverns under the Institute or about traveling into the past of other timelines.

Dawn nodded. "She loves foren-sic historical research through old files. Did her dissertation on the techniques of forensic historical research."

"Wow," Duster said. "No wonder she's been on our list."

Dawn nodded. "If anyone can find evidence of who this Tombstone Dan is or was or what even happened to him, Professor Lund should be able to do it."

"Keep us informed," Duster said.

"Looking forward to meeting her," Bonnie said.

Duster shook his head. "Just when you think you know every little detail about a historical place, something like this comes up."

"I just can't believe we never heard of a man going by Tombstone Dan in that valley," Dawn said. "The name alone would have made him memorable."

And since she and Madison had lived hundreds of lifetimes in the Monumental Lodge above the valley and on the main trail in and out of the place, not knowing some-one in the valley seemed impossible. It was enough to drive a historian like her crazy.

"If he played poker in those casinos," Duster said, "I'll recognize him when I see him. You want me to go back and try to see if I can spot him?"

Dawn shook her head. "Not yet, unless you are planning a trip back. I think our best chance is Professor Lund. And this is a great excuse to get her on board."

Both Bonnie and Duster nodded.

If Professor Lund was as good as people said she was, Tombstone Dan would soon be revealed.

So, as Dawn finished her sandwich, she and Bonnie and Duster worked to figure out a way to get Professor Lund to join them.

Dawn had a hunch that wasn't going to be an easy task.

ONE

August 20th, 2018
Madison, Wisconsin

PROFESSOR MARGARET LUND, Maggie to her friends, sat at a colorful yellow metal table on the huge concrete patio of the Union at the University of Wisconsin, Madison. The patio was called the Union Terrace and it looked out over a wide and beautifully calm lake. This morning the surface of the lake almost looked like a mirror. For an early August morning, the humidity was still low and the temperature was perfect.

A slight mist hung over the lake that she knew would clear in the next bit of time as the sun came fully up. Around her was the smell of coffee and eggs and bacon. Her coffee sitting in front of her was still too hot to drink.

She had dressed in a light cotton blouse with a jogging bra under it, jeans, and tennis shoes. She had brought a wide-brimmed hat for later to protect her freckled face and neck, but the sun wasn't high enough yet to worry about that too much, so her hat sat on the chair beside her. A little sun did her good at times, even though too much turned her into a red lobster.

That always seemed to be her fate with her red hair, fair white skin, and freckles. Even though she had been a professor for almost five years now, most of the students still thought of her as a student because she kept her red hair long and she dressed like a student. And the freckles on her nose and neck made her look even younger.

She loved coming to the Union Terrace just as the sun came up, drinking a cup of coffee, reading the newspaper on her pad, and then looking over her notes from the previous day on her research.

She had just started to dig into the major historical families of the Midwest, with the idea of writing a book about many of them. But the project was still new and it still didn't have a shape for her. She hoped the research would give it some.

Around her there were very few students since the term was still a ways from starting for the fall and summer school had finished. Some of the freshmen had arrived but they were too busy to sit around on the Terrace.

She considered this one of the top times in the city.

"Excuse us," a woman's voice said and Maggie turned to look up at a woman who looked to be about Maggie's age with long brown hair pulled back and a friendly smile. She wore a silk blouse and jeans and seemed very at ease with everything, so clearly not a student.

Standing beside her was a guy about the same age, handsome, wearing a plaid western-style shirt, jeans and a cowboy hat. He was standing back slightly from the woman. He looked like he belonged on the cover of a western novel as the hero.

"Sorry to bother you on such a wonderful morning," the woman said. "My name is Dawn Edwards and this is Madison Rogers. Would you mind if we talked with you for a moment?"

It took Maggie's mind what seemed like a long instant before she realized just who these two people were.

Oh, my, God! They were two of the most respected and famous historians of all time. And two of the best historical researchers that had ever lived.

"Oh, heavens," Maggie said. "Please."

She waved a limp-wristed hand as best she could at the other two metal chairs at the table.

She was amazed she even got those words out of her mouth. Some day she had hoped to meet these two, but now to have them just walk up and ask to join her stunned her to her core.

What in the world were they doing here? They lived out west somewhere, she was sure.

As the two sat at the table with her, Dr. Rogers said, "Wow, this is really beautiful here."

"Stunning," Dr. Edwards said, looking with her husband out over the water and the thin mist that floated above it.

Then Dr. Edwards turned back to Maggie. "Again, sorry to bother you."

Maggie managed to wave a hand. "I am a big fan of both of your work and had hoped to meet you some day."

Actually anyone in historical research hoped to meet Dr. Edwards or Dr. Rogers. Now Maggie was getting to meet them both at the same moment.

"I'm surprised we haven't met before now, actually," Dr. Rogers said. "Your thesis on the methods of forensic record research is a must-read for anyone thinking of researching any historical event."

Maggie was sure that she blushed. She blushed a lot, again the fate of fair skin and red hair.

"I can't agree more," Dr. Edwards said.

Maggie flat didn't know what to say and was a little angry at herself for being so in awe of these two that she was having trouble talking. Her friends thought of her as almost terminally shy and at the moment she was proving it.

Dr. Edwards smiled and seemed to understand, thankfully just going on.

"We're here with an offer," Dr. Edwards said. "I would imagine you know about the Historical Research Institute in Boise, Idaho?"

Maggie nodded. She knew the Institute did amazing things in support and funding for historical researchers. She had never felt she had a project worth applying for a grant from the Institute yet.

"We are major backers of the Institute," Dr. Edwards said.

"I had heard that," Maggie said, thankful that she could actually get some words out.

"But basically, why we are here," Dr. Edwards said, "is that I personally need your help on a research project."

"My help?" Maggie asked, very glad her voice didn't squeak.

"I don't know if you are familiar with the books I did about a mining town called Roosevelt, Idaho?"

"I am," Maggie said. "Honestly read both of them twice trying to figure out how you managed to get such crisp and clear details into the writing and descriptions."

"Thank you," Dr. Edwards said, smiling. "Well, I just discovered something about that town that has me completely stumped and I need someone with your forensic research abilities to help me dig it out."

"I am flattered," Maggie said.

Actually, she was stunned and excited, but was doing her best to somehow contain those feelings.

"We would like to make you an offer," Dr. Rogers said. "Come to the Institute for a year in Boise, all expenses paid and a nice salary on top of that. After that you can decide if you want to stay or come back here to teaching."

Maggie shook her head. "I have classes starting next month. It would be difficult, if not impossible for me to change that."

Plus what she didn't say was that she didn't want to take any chance of losing her teaching position here at the university.

"The Institute has already talked with the chairman of your department," Dr. Edwards said, smiling. "If you decide to take this job for a year, your position here will be held while you are gone."

"How—?"

Dr. Rogers smiled. "We and the Institute have an enormous amount of money and pull. In fact, your chairman thinks it would be a real benefit for the department to have an alum from the Institute teaching."

Dr. Edwards laughed. "That's true, and we also sort of bribed them. If you decide to take this research job working with me for a year, Madison and I will fund two chairs in the department and agree to visit and lecture."

Maggie opened her mouth, but not even a sound came out so she closed it. This must all be a dream and she would wake up in bed at any point with the alarm going off.

Dr. Rogers waved his hand and laughed. "We're going to do that anyway. But the idea of tying it to you coming to work with us sort of was inferred. But the two chairs will be funded no matter what you decide."

Dr. Edwards looked directly at Maggie, whose wide brown eyes were clear and very intense.

"I would love working with you for a year on this project," Dr. Edwards said. "And I think you will find the Institute an amazing place, with stunning resources. Especially for the kind of work you do."

Dr. Rogers put a card on the table in front of Maggie with a phone number on it. "Give it some thought. We would arrange all moving and pay for your apartment here for a year as well, so you wouldn't lose it."

"Thank you for this amazing offer," Maggie said. "As you can tell, I am speechless."

The two famous historians stood, both smiling.

"We'll be here until tomorrow morning if you want to talk some more," Dr. Rogers said.

"I really hope you join me on this project," Dr. Edwards said. "I could really use your help and the two of us could really produce a great book or two out of what we find, I'm sure."

With that they turned and headed back across the Terrace through the colorful metal tables toward the Union building.

Maggie watched the two great researchers walk away, then looked at the card in front of her.

At any moment now the alarm would go off and this amazing, wonderful dream would be over.

Instead, she just sat there, staring at the card and thinking until the warmth of the sun's rays finally caught her attention and she packed up and headed back inside before she burned.

TWO

Monumental Creek
Central Idaho
July, 1899

DAN GRAY, FORMERLY of Kansas City, now living pretty much everywhere in the West, let Jenny, his horse, lead him at her own pace up a game trail along a stream that was called Monumental Creek on a rough map. The stream looked like it might have some nice trout in it and maybe tonight, after he made camp, he would see what he could catch for dinner.

Nothing beat the taste of fresh, pan-fried trout in the evening.

The mountains towered over him on both sides, in many places higher than he could see. The slopes of those mountains were so vertical it would be impossible to climb out. Not exactly canyon walls, but they might as well have been.

The valley alternated between fairly wide between the steep slopes and very narrow. At the moment it felt wide. Tall stands of mountain pine were around him, broken by small meadows of knee-high grass.

The smell was of hot pine needles and there was only a slight breeze moving the hot air.

Above the trees, the towering mountains still had some snow at the tallest peaks even though it was July. But down in the deep valley where he was, especially for the hours the sun got to the bottom of the valley, the air was warm, so warm he had taken off his top coat a few miles back and rode only in his rolled-up shirt sleeves.

He had stopped a few times to splash cold snow-melt stream water on his face and neck and over his head.

He kept a wet bandana covering his neck under his cowboy hat and at the moment it was about dried out.

A person looking at him, Dan knew, would think he was just another broke mountain man, working to eke out some food and find a little color in the streams to buy supplies when he needed them. With his dark beard, longish dark hair, and sun-red skin, he looked older than his thirty-two years.

Actually, Dan was far more than he looked. He originally had been born in Kansas City, in the future from where he was at now, in 1990 under the name Dan Silver. He had a number of doctorate degrees in different aspects of the history and science of cattle ranching.

He had applied to the Historical Institute in late 2019 and had been offered the ability to go back in other timelines in early 2020. He had spent over a thousand years now in the past in just a few months of real time, mostly around the Kansas City area and down into Texas, doing research for his books.

Because of his knowledge of the business, in this time period he had become a stupidly wealthy cattleman at a very young age. Actually, he had done the same thing in the last ten times back.

This time, he had gotten bored, very bored with the cattle business after just a year or so. That surprised him. He had decided that he needed a break.

He had needed something different and west, beyond the Rockies, called to him like a lost lover. He had always just gone right from the Institute east to Kansas City each trip back. He had never spent any real time out west.

And he had been right. The more he explored, the more he realized that the Old West was just about as different as it got from cattle country, especially in the late 1890s.

Before he headed west, without his business partner knowing, he had transferred enough money into a dozen western banks along the West Coast to be rich the rest of this life in this timeline, told his partner the business was his to do with as he pleased, signed it all over, mounted up and headed out.

In two winters and one summer now, he had kept moving and never regretted for a moment his decision. He had no real idea what he was looking for, but he believed he would know it when he found it.

He knew deep down though that what he was really looking for more than anything was just a place to live, a place to claim as his own and build a home in this timeline, and maybe in other timelines going forward.

He wanted a place he could just be alone and write and read for some years.

Plus, he wanted to build the home himself, no matter how long it took. He clearly had the years to do it. And he had come to love not only the Victorian style of the Institute building in Boise, but some of the fantastic mansions in Kansas City.

To him, those homes looked like perfect comfort.

Ahead of him and Jenny, the steep-walled canyon widened slightly into a meadow and Dan got off and let her graze as he went to splash more water on his face and get his bandana wet again.

He was in the Monumental Valley, which in a few years would be the site of a massive gold rush, the last one on the continent. He wasn't sure why he came to this valley. More to just see it before man ruined it than anything else.

He knew that Dawn and Madison and Duster and Bonnie, the four who ran the Historical Institute, would spend a lot of timelines here in this valley in coming years. He really had no desire to run into them. So far, in over a thousand years, he had only actually bumped into one other historical traveler that he knew about.

Of course, in 2020, there were only just over thirty historical travelers, going back into other timelines. He sure didn't know them all. Even if he had seen their face in the library in 2020, they would look very different here in the past. Context of where a person is at is everything.

Plus back here everyone aged. It was often tough to recognize someone you knew at thirty-five when they are seventy.

As the cold water ran down his back and he wiped off his face and put the bandana on his neck, he saw the canyon through the trees.

Or at least thought he saw the canyon.

Over the years in the cattle business, a cowboy got used to losing cattle up small side canyons, often canyons hidden from view of those in the main canyon.

A canyon like that would show up face-on as nothing more than what looked like a crack in a rock wall. But if you went up to the wall, you could see part of the wall was much father out than the other part, forming a path or corridor that went off from the main canyon at almost a ninety-degree angle.

There were canyons all over the southwest marked "hidden canyon" on the maps if they were near known cattle drive routes. Those hidden canyons could make cattle just seemingly vanish. And make a cattleman's profit vanish just as fast.

In his hundreds of years on the trails early on in his research in the past, he had checked out more hidden canyons than he wanted to think about.

He studied the rock wall across the narrow valley. From where he was at, it sure looked like a hidden canyon opening.

He finished filling his canteen with the bitingly-cold fresh water, splashed more on his face and neck, then took off his bandana, soaked it again and put it back on his neck, sending shivers down his spine.

Then he let Jenny drink a little before he mounted up and splashed across the stream through the pine trees toward the canyon wall.

There was no trail, not even game trails, so he had to do a little bushwhacking through some brush under the trees.

Less than five minutes later, he discovered he had been right.

He was facing the opening to a hidden canyon.

Anyone moving along the stream as he had been doing would never see the entrance unless they got lucky like he had and knew what they were looking for.

The canyon opening was wide enough to get a wagon through with moving just a few loose rocks.

He dismounted and tied up Jenny in the shade, then started up the canyon through the rocks on foot. After about a hundred paces, the canyon turned to the right, framed by high rock cliffs on both sides and a small stream coming down the middle.

He felt like he was walking in a massive hallway. Only minutes of sun every day ever hit the bottom of this narrow canyon, which explained why there was so little brush.

He could also feel himself getting excited.

Really excited.

Then, after another hundred paces, the narrow, rock-walled canyon opened up into what looked to be an almost round meadow, with rock walls on all sides and a waterfall cascading down the far canyon wall.

Stands of pine filled part of the valley floor and a small beaver pond backed up some of the water, creating a bright blue pond right in front of him.

Above him, the towering mountains seemed to guard over the small box-canyon meadow.

Standing there, staring at the beauty, he knew instantly he had found a home.

THREE

August 20th, 2018
Madison, Wisconsin

IT WASN'T EVEN eight in the morning when Maggie called her department head. She had at least waited until she was back in her wonderful second-floor apartment in an old Victorian mansion.

Her apartment was the entire second floor and she loved it, including the furniture she had found to furnish it.

Someday she would own and furnish her own Victorian mansion, but for now having the entire second story of one as an apartment was more than enough. And the Institute offering to pay her rent for a year so she wouldn't lose this place was wonderful.

Her department head's name was Dr. Jeff Hudson. Maggie had been friends with Jeff and his wife and their two wonderful kids for five years now. She trusted Jeff more than anyone, including her sister back in New York.

Since her parents had died, she and her sister only talked about once a month. Sometimes not even that often. Her sister was having marriage problems, job problems, and drinking problems. Anything Maggie did or said seemed to make things worse instead of help.

Jeff just laughed as he picked up the phone. "I was wondering when you were going to call. What did you think of Dr. Edwards and Dr. Rogers?"

"They were more than I imagined them to be," Maggie said.

"Did you get a word out?" Jeff asked, laughing.

He knew her shyness far too well. "Barely. And it wasn't funny."

That made Jeff laugh even harder.

"They offered me a job working with Dr. Edwards on a project at the Institute in Boise."

"I know," Jeff said. "They talked with me first about you having the ability to come back after a year and about our ability to cover your classes on short notice this fall."

"Can I and can you?" Maggie asked, feeling her stomach twist. This really was the key element in her deciding on this job.

"Your teaching position will be here for your return," Jeff said. "And covering your classes this fall won't be an issue."

"Dr. Rogers said that the two chairs they offered to fund would happen if I said yes or no."

Jeff laughed. "I know that. And I also know that it is your work that has helped this department gain reputation to attract their money in the first place."

"So you wouldn't mind?" Maggie asked, not really believing that this might even be happening.

"I would want you to call me regularly," Jeff said. "And the kids would miss you. But otherwise, I think it is an opportunity you can't pass up."

Maggie took a deep breath and nodded to herself.

"Thanks," she said. "I think I'm going to call them and accept."

"Sure you just don't want to go to their hotel and nod silently?" Jeff asked, laughing.

"Not funny," she said, laughing and feeling the tension of the last hour drain away.

"Oh, yes it is," Jeff said. "Now hang up and call them. I got you covered here."

"Thank you," Maggie said.

Jeff just laughed and hung up.

And before she could lose her nerve, she called the number Dr. Rogers had left.

Dr. Edwards answered the phone. "Great to hear from you. Do you have some questions?"

"Dr. Edwards," Maggie said, "I would love to accept your offer."

"Fantastic," Dr. Edwards said.

Maggie was pleased that Dr. Edwards sounded genuinely happy with the news.

"Would you like to meet for an early lunch in a couple hours, say eleven, and talk about the details? We saw this nifty little café called Downtown on State Street. Looks like yummy pizza."

"I would love that," Maggie said. "And their pizza is to die for."

"Fantastic," Dr. Edwards said. "And it's Dawn. Call me Dawn."

"My friends call me Maggie."

"Perfect, Maggie," Dawn said. "See you in two hours."

Maggie clicked off her phone and just stared at it for a moment.

The dream continued and so far no alarm had woken her up.

For the next year, her life had just changed.

Just that fast.

And that had her more excited than she wanted to admit.

FOUR

Off of Monumental Creek
Central Idaho
July, 1899

IT WAS THREE days later, while exploring the hidden box canyon to make sure he had every foot of it measured so that he could record it down in Boise, that Dan found the old camp.

At the highest part at the back of the canyon away from the entrance, on the upper edge of the trees, on a small rock ledge, were the remains of a trapper's camp.

Dan almost missed it because he was paying attention to how the view back over the entire small canyon looked and the beautiful waterfall to his right.

Tattered bedding and faded leather saddlebags still remained in the camp, along with some supplies. Rocks had been piled up for a fire and weeds had grown up through the bedding.

Clearly the camp had been abandoned here for five or six years. It looked like it had been set up as a winter's camp with shelter from the snow under a rock outcropping. He had seen numbers of those in the last few years of riding the west.

But something had happened here. The saddlebags and supplies should not still be here.

To the right of the ledge and down a dozen steps, just in the trees, Dan found the remains of a skeleton of a horse, one bullet hole through its skull. It looked like a mountain cat had worked at the remains of the horse at first, then the birds and mice and sun had taken care of the rest over the years.

At that point Dan knew what had happened.

He kept searching and finally near the camp, under what appeared to be a form of lean-to shelter made out of cut pine that had collapsed over the years, Dan found the old trapper, not much more than a skeleton.

He had an old pistol across his lap and had clearly shot himself in the head as well. A saddle rifle lay beside him, one of his hands still holding it.

It made Dan sick to his stomach, but it was not the first time he had seen death and not the first time he had seen what the loneliness of the vast Midwest plains and the rugged western mountains could do to a person.

You had to really love the loneliness, embrace it like a friend, or it would crush you like a rockslide.

Clearly this man had been crushed by it.

Dan had no doubt that the long winters in these steep mountains must be extreme. More than likely the sun wouldn't reach these deep valley floors for a month at a time. That would be hard on anyone with the wrong frame of mind.

Dan spent the next day digging the old trapper a grave near the remains of his horse.

He felt that if he was going to live in this small valley, then he needed to give its first resident a proper burial.

When Dan had the remains of the trapper down about four feet and covered with dirt and rocks, he spent some hours along the cliff face until he found a large, flat rock that would work as a tombstone.

Dan spent part of the next morning burying one end of the rock in the dirt at the head of the grave so that the flat rock would stand against the weather.

Then, carefully, taking two more days, Dan had chiseled on the flat rock the rough words, "Rest in Peace."

He would keep the area clear of brush over the years that he planned on living here.

That night, as he sat around his campfire, planning what to do next, he realized that the name of this canyon needed to be Tombstone Canyon, in honor of the trapper who had found it.

A week later, Dan left the hidden canyon and headed back down the main canyon along Monumental Creek. He now had a purpose for the first time in years.

He had found a home.

Now he had to build a shelter.

It took him four days to get to Boise to register his mining claim in the canyon and purchase the land around the claim inside the rock walls.

He paid with cash and signed all the papers Tombstone Dan, getting a magistrate to make it his legal signature just in case any of the people from his old life in Kansas City were looking for Dan Gray.

He doubted they were, but better safe than sorry.

Dan Gray was officially dead for all intents and purposes, even though he still had a lot of money in banks in the west under that name.

A week later, with three pack-horses loaded with supplies and equipment to survive the winter and build the first part of his home, he headed back to Tombstone Canyon.

It had been years since he had felt this excited. He knew he had a hard winter ahead in those high mountains of Idaho.

But he would survive it, he had no doubt.

And he would start the process of building a home he had always wanted to build.

FIVE

August 23rd, 2018
Boise, Idaho

MAGGIE LOOKED AT the piece of paper in her hand with the address on it, then back up at the gate and the large Victorian mansion behind it. On the stone wall was a brass plaque that said, Historical Research Institute.

How in the world could that be? She flat loved Victorian homes and it turned out that the Institute was in a Victorian home. How could that even be possible?

Of course, none of this was possible.

The last three days had been a whirlwind of activity. Dawn and Madison had left early and headed back, then yesterday Maggie had closed up her apartment and gone to the airport with Jeff's help carrying luggage and some boxes to be met by a private jet that was to pick her up.

Jeff had just laughed when he saw the jet and said, "Wow, are you getting the red carpet treatment."

All Maggie could do was shake her head in amazement. Things like this were never supposed to happen to university professors.

She was the only person on the plane besides two women pilots, both older than she was, and a very nice guy named Ben who seemed to be a steward. He served her a wonderful lunch of fresh salad and ham sandwiches, plus iced tea.

Ben looked to be about her age and was tall enough that he could have played basketball except for his very thick glasses. He wore dress slacks and a tan dress shirt with running shoes. His hair was short and dark and his eyes behind his glasses were green and penetrating.

She found him amazingly attractive, which surprised her considering that her world was in the process of being tipped on end.

Over the last few years she had dated a few times, but being a college professor sort of cut off a lot of possible dates, since she would never date a student and she never had much chance to meet the people outside the university.

Besides, she had been busy and relationships took time. She had told Jeff that once and he had just laughed, as he seemed to do a lot at her expense. Then he had said simply, "You just haven't met the right one yet."

She hoped he was right.

Ben might not be the right one, but he sure looked like he would be fun to have a fling with. She would have to figure out the Institute rules on that sort of thing.

Maggie had managed to get past her shyness enough to ask him how he liked working for the Institute. He had just laughed and said, "There is no place better."

Otherwise, he sat up near the pilots giving her privacy and she just read and wondered the entire three-hour flight what she had gotten into.

As luck would have it, Ben's job was not only to be the steward on the plane, but to get her to her wonderful two-story, two-bedroom condo on the Boise River, show her how everything worked, get her a special Institute card that worked as door key and a credit card just about anywhere in town, and help her get groceries into her new place.

He did all that, driving her around in a large, brand new white Cadillac SUV that belonged to the Institute. He said he would show her how she could get and use a car exactly like it later on.

Sure, university professors drove a brand new Cadillac all the time. Sure.

Then he gave her an address and directions on how to get along the path beside the river to the Institute or she could walk up the sidewalk along the streets for a meeting at nine in the morning with Dawn.

He had also given her specific instructions to not dress in anything but her normal professor work clothes. Jeans and tennis shoes were the normal attire for the institute.

Maggie had been very glad to hear that.

Damn she was attracted to him. And he seemed drawn to her as well. Not only was this new job going to be fun, meeting people like Ben was going to be a side benefit she hadn't even considered.

After Ben left, she had unpacked, explored her condo a little, then had cooked herself a light meal and just sat on her patio, staring in wonder as hundreds, if not thousands of people, floated past on the river on anything that might float. It was like watching a continuous moving party.

Clearly Boise had some fun aspects about it. Who knew?

And she really loved how, as the sun started to set, the evening cooled down. That was a real benefit she hadn't known about either. In the Midwest the heat and mugginess just kept on.

Also here, the air was crisp and clear. In Madison, the air often had a haze to it that was all the humidity, sort of dulling everything down. She loved the crispness, she had to admit.

At that moment she realized there had been no humidity all day. Not a bit. Just a dry heat.

She had found heaven. A beautiful condo, clear air, no humidity, good looking men, all expenses paid, a big salary, and new Cadillacs to drive.

Yup, this was heaven.

Now, the next morning, as rested and as excited as a tired woman could be, she stood in jeans, tennis shoes, a cotton blouse, and light summer jacket in front

of a classic Victorian mansion surrounded and shaded by tall oak and willow trees. Two other Victorian mansions were on either side of it and from the looks of it, the mansion grounds went all the way down to the path along the river.

Looking at every detail, she went through the gate and onto the grounds, noting how the green grass alternated with flowing flowerbeds, all blooming in different colors with flowers she didn't recognize.

The white-painted wooden front steps actually creaked a little as she went up to the wide, wooden front porch with period furniture in two groupings on both sides of the massive wooden front door.

Not a detail was wrong for the 1880 through 1890 time period this home must have been built in.

A small brass sign beside the door said, "Please come in."

She turned the old door handle and pushed hard on the large door. Again, not a detail was missed.

A perfect building to be the face of an organization that did historical research. If there was a detail wrong, she would have been surprised.

And inside the cooler main room, the attention to detail continued.

Massive cloth drapes in floral patterns from the time period hung down beside the two tall windows in the front room, pulled back by thick cords to allow the light to stream in through the white sheer coverings. A dark maple staircase with an ornate banister led to an upper floor.

The floors in the main room were wide planked and stained dark and also looked to be maple.

The lights in ornate white sconces on the walls looked to have been original oil lamps, but had been converted to electrical without losing their charm.

The couch and two chairs in front of a massive stone fireplace were also perfect period furniture.

Not a detail had been missed.

"Pretty amazing place, huh?" Dawn said, coming down the staircase. She had her long brown hair pulled back and was dressed almost exactly as she had been in Madison. Jeans, a beautiful blouse, and running shoes.

"Every detail is perfect to the late 1880s," Maggie said, indicating the room around her.

"Thank you," Dawn said. "We work to keep it accurate. Glad you noticed."

Dawn indicated that they should sit in front of the fireplace and Maggie sat on the couch while Dawn took the high-backed, overstuffed chair closest to where Maggie was sitting.

The room was still cool, but Maggie had no doubt that unless they had hidden air conditioning, this room would be warm in the afternoon.

"I thought I would tell you a little about the project I need help on," Dawn said. "Then in about fifteen minutes, Ben is going to be here to show you the library and where your office will be and introduce you to the others."

"Wonderful," Maggie said. "And thank you for the fantastic ride out from Wisconsin and for the condo."

"Least we can do," Dawn said. "Anything you need at all, just call Ben. If he's not available, he will get someone to help you."

Maggie nodded. "I'm pretty independent, so once I catch on where things are, I'll be fine."

And she would be too. But right now she was very relieved to hear that Ben would be available for the thousand questions she already had building. Better to bother him than Dawn.

Plus, it didn't hurt to spend time with a guy so damned good-looking.

"So here is what I have run into," Dawn said. "I have on your desk in your new office all the paperwork I have found so far on a man by the name of Tombstone Dan. Sadly, it's not much."

"Interesting name," Maggie said.

"It is and I'm pretty sure it just came into being around 1889 in Boise, but I don't know for sure."

"So besides his name, what makes this man so special?" Maggie asked.

"It turns out that we think he might have owned the six major saloons in Roosevelt, Idaho," Dawn said. "And up until six months ago, I didn't know that, he kept it so well hidden."

"Any history about the man?"

"Nothing I can find," Dawn said, shaking her head. "No pictures. Nothing."

Maggie could hear the frustration in Dawn's voice. Clearly this man with the strange name suddenly appearing in history, in a town Dawn knew better than anyone alive, was bothering her.

Maggie had to admit, it would have bothered her as well.

"I'm thinking we both work at this from different angles," Dawn said, "and every week we have a meeting and compare notes and findings and brainstorm which direction to head next."

"Sounds like a perfect plan," Maggie said.

At that moment Ben came in from the back of the building and Dawn stood, so Maggie did as well.

"Ben is one of our top librarians," Dawn said. "He knows our resources better than anyone and can help you get settled in your office. Each librarian is assigned to a researcher and you work in teams as much or as little as you need. Ben has been assigned to work with you."

"Librarian?" Maggie said, smiling at the tall, handsome man. "You didn't tell me that."

"My job is to help the researchers here with anything they need," Ben said, smiling back at her. "And it is an honor to help you get settled in. I have been a fan of your work for years now. Your thesis changed how a lot of us look at historical research here. So any help I can give you will be my pleasure."

All Maggie could do was blush.

Dawn just laughed, but it was a friendly, understanding laugh.

SIX

Tombstone Canyon
Central Idaho
May, 1900

DAN HAD FINISHED his first rough cabin with a stone fireplace the previous fall just as the first snow flew. He had also built a shelter for his horses among the trees down by the meadow and stream.

He had decided this first cabin would end up being just storage and a workshop for him later. He would build his real home, a Victorian mansion, on a ledge on the right side of the canyon as you entered, with a view of not only the mountains and the rising sun to the east, but of the entrance to the canyon.

Safer that way, even though he never expected anyone to find this canyon. But the trapper had and he had, so someone else might.

As he expected, the winter had been long and hard and he kept busy mostly just making sure Jenny and his other horses were doing all right. Plus he had to keep clearing the snow from around his small cabin doors and one window.

On some days, just the hundred-yard hike down to his horses had taken him an hour through the snow.

But the canyon was small enough to be sheltered from any high winds and the snow didn't get that deep compared to some more open places he had seen.

So he weathered the winter fine. And actually got some writing done on his next book about cattle country. More than likely, it would be his last book on that topic.

Then, in May, as he knew it would, the weather cleared.

He had his main home plan all worked out over the long winter's nights. He had always loved the Victorian mansion look of the homes being built back east. And the Victorian mansion that was the headquarters of the Institute in 2020 he loved. He wondered if he might be able to come close to that look here.

It would be two stories with a massive fireplace on either end of the building. Both bedrooms upstairs would have a fireplace and the living room and the back bedroom downstairs would have one as well. He had a lot of study to do on how to build and vent fireplaces, but that was possible to do.

He even worked out how he could get some running water to the home from the waterfall area, so he planned an indoor toilet and an outhouse as well just in case.

And he would set up a generator in the stream for electricity.

As soon as he thought it was safe, he and Jenny and his packhorses headed out of Tombstone Canyon and down the rushing Monumental Creek. This time it took him just over a week to get to Boise, but he

made it. Next year he would wait another week or two to start, give the snow more time to melt off and the streams to recede.

In Boise, he spent the first full month coming to understand that without some real training, he would never be able to build the home he wanted to build on his own.

But he wasn't in a hurry. He had the time to train, and it might take him a few lifetimes back here to get it right, but he could do it.

So he spent a month learning about how to build a solid rock foundation for his home, and the two solid fireplaces his plan would need. He also had an architect look over his plan and make sure it was sound, drawing up the images.

Then Dan went back into his canyon with supplies and tools enough to get through the summer.

He saw no one and by the time fall rolled around, he had built a large stone foundation for his home and two towering rock fireplaces with two openings in each, one on the main floor, one where the second floor would be.

By the time the first snow flew, he was back in Boise staying at the Boise Hotel for the winter.

Two things happened that winter and this trip back turned once again.

He took lessons in fine home building from two master craftsmen in town, including helping them on the construction of two Victorian-style homes in the north end of the city.

And he came to love the game of poker.

He spent his days learning construction, his nights learning poker. He used the name Daniel Gregory in the poker rooms just to be safe from both the Daniel Gray name and the Tombstone Dan name.

And along the way, he also came to really appreciate the attitude in saloons in the west compared to the cowboy bars back in cattle country.

Most of the western saloon owners kept their bars clean and free of disturbances.

Dan liked that.

And as Dan did with anything he set his mind to, he became good at both construction and poker.

He also learned the saloon business, something that he found interesting, far more than the business of cattle. Maybe saloons of the old west would be his next research topic.

And the more he thought about that, the more he liked that idea. And in 2020, no one had yet done that book that he knew of.

The following spring, with four packhorses loaded with supplies, he headed back into the mountains and his canyon.

He felt more driven, more alive than he had at any time in his past. And the high mountain air only helped that.

By the time the summer was finished, he had milled the lumber and the first floor of his home was framed up. He had built a temporary roof over the construction and sealed up everything for the winter. It still wasn't finished by a long ways, but what he had worked on all summer would withstand the snow and cold.

He had also built his front porch and the view from his large front porch looking out over the small box canyon and at the mountains to the east was breathtaking.

He could imagine no better place to be.

After two years of working on the house now, he was more excited than ever to keep going.

He planned on spending one more winter in Boise and work next summer on the second story and get the roof on, then spend the winter working on the interior of his new home. He would keep living in his smaller log cabin until he had it finished.

But on the way out, he ran across some placer miners along Monumental Creek.

And they were all finding color.

It was time for the big gold rush to start this next spring into this area.

The winter weather was about to shut the miners down, but he knew what that meant for next spring. Monumental Creek would be flooded with miners and Roosevelt, the town that would end up being the center of this gold rush would spring up.

He didn't worry about anyone finding his hidden canyon. Not only was it naturally protected, but he had it posted and he owned both the land and the claims.

So once he made it back to Boise, he dug into the records and realized that the plat for the town of Roosevelt had already been laid out and parcels were being bought.

Roosevelt would be just over two miles below the mouth of his canyon.

And for as long as the gold rush existed, he would have company close by.

For some reason, he didn't mind that.

That night, while sitting in a poker game in the wonderful downstairs poker room of the new Idanha Hotel, he came up with what he needed to do.

The next day he purchased six of the parcels along the main street of the new town of Roosevelt, spread the length of the town. He set up a consortium under three businessmen's names to be the official owners.

Then he first headed to Seattle to draw money out of his Dan Gray account there and then went by ship on down to San Francisco to draw money from a bank he had put money in there as well.

Over the winter in Boise, he put a number of building crews together because they knew him from his building training the previous winter and liked him and besides, he paid well.

The next spring, as soon as they could get into the valley after the snow melted, his building crews descended on the new town of Roosevelt and by the time the summer was over, they had built six saloons and stocked them.

And all six had pianos, hauled in by mules in pieces since no wagons could get into Roosevelt.

And besides a few of the construction foremen and the official paperwork in Boise, no one in Roosevelt knew he owned the saloons. He had set up a company headquartered in Boise to run them and to build more around the west from the profits coming out of Roosevelt.

Nothing like a saloon in a mining boomtown to rake in the money. He really was going to write that historical books about the old west saloons. Maybe more than one.

His only command to those who ran the saloons was that the saloons be kept clean, that each had a piano, and that each had poker tables. He let the managers of the company he set up do the rest.

Three years later, as he finished the last details on his home in Tombstone Canyon, he was far, far richer than he had ever gotten being as a cattleman.

And that winter, for the first time, he stayed in his new home in Tombstone Canyon. And only a few times did he go down to Roosevelt to play some poker, again using the name Daniel Gregory when asked or introducing himself.

He also knew that two time travelers ran the general store in Roosevelt, but they didn't know him because they had come back from a time before he joined the research part of the Institute.

And he had even seen Duster twice going into a saloon. That night Dan had gone to a different saloon to play poker. He saw no point in announcing he was here to anyone.

PART TWO
A Puzzle

SEVEN

June 1st, 2019
Monumental Summit, Idaho

MAGGIE SAT ALONE on the balcony of the massive Monumental Summit Lodge and stared out over the valley below and the hundreds of miles of the Idaho mountains and primitive area in front of her.

In all her life she had never imagined a view so spectacular, especially with the setting sun coloring the tops of mountains in shades of pink and orange and red. Many of the mountains were still capped in snow even though it was June.

The air had a slight bite to it, but it felt great after the warm day in Boise and the drive up here.

Refreshing.

She felt as if she belonged here.

Living in Wisconsin and being born just outside of New York, she never would have thought she would love the high mountains of Idaho. But she had taken to them like they had always been home.

All her life she had felt a pull to go west, just never had until last summer when Dawn had invited her to join the Institute.

All fall and winter in Boise, Maggie had been working side by side with Ben, trying to find information about a man who owned the bars in an old mining town that had boomed and died in the valley below the lodge.

Just a few miles from where she sat, actually.

Through the fall, Maggie and Ben had gotten along perfectly, and had managed to even hold off the intense physical attraction until November when they both finally just decided to go for it.

Maggie felt as if Ben's massive intellect and ability to see patterns fit perfectly with her ability to dig out details that all others would miss. They were a great team and great in bed together, but by the spring both of them had decided to just be friends and cool the relationship side.

Ben had seemed to be perfect for her, but for both of them there was just something missing. And they were both smart enough to know it.

But she still loved working with him every day and they talked as old friends. In fact, he even told her about a wonderful woman he had met while skiing in March and for Maggie it had felt like a relief.

Ben had an undergraduate degree in mathematics, but had discovered his love for historical research and the workings of libraries outweighed his love of math and he had ended up with a doctorate in library science. It was the combination of math and library science that had drawn Bonnie and Duster Kendal's attention to him and they had hired him.

Bonnie and Duster were the top two mathematical minds in the world and with Dawn and Madison and Director Parks helped run the institute. Maggie had only met Bonnie and Duster once in passing and they both seemed so normal for such famous and brilliant people.

Maggie and Dawn also got along wonderfully through the winter, once Maggie got over being star-struck working for such a famous historian. Dawn and her wonderful sense of humor made that easy, thankfully.

It had taken all winter and most of the spring before Maggie finally made a breakthrough on the mystery man named Tombstone Dan.

That guy, without a doubt, had been smart and had covered his tracks well. But the Institute had access to resources like no others and with Ben's help, Maggie had found the origin of Tombstone Dan.

It seems his original name had been Dan Gray, a young and very rich cattleman from Kansas City. In 1898, at the age of thirty, he had left his business to his partner and disappeared into the west.

Maggie had been able to track numbers of bank accounts belonging to Dan Gray around the west. And he had had a lot of money, for the time, in banks all the way from the Mexican border to the Canadian border.

In 1900, a year before gold was discovered in the Monumental Creek in the valley below this lodge, Dan had legally changed his name to Tombstone Dan and filed a mining claim and bought all the land in a small side canyon off of the valley below.

Then through a land and investment company set up in Boise, as Roosevelt was formed, he bought parcels on the main street of Roosevelt and showed up at spring melt as the miners were pouring into the valley and built six saloons.

There was no record at all of what happened to him when the town went under water in the spring of 1909.

No one was killed since the town had taken days to flood. Much of the furniture in the saloons and all of the pianos were saved and carted out before the town went under. In fact, from what she had found out, five of the six saloons had shut down the fall before the flood and all the furniture and supplies worth saving had been taken out of the valley.

By that point in time, Tombstone Dan's investment business owned fifty different saloons up and down the west coast and he was a very, very rich man.

Under the name Tombstone Dan.

He still had money as Dan Gray and money as Tombstone Dan.

There was no record of either name surfacing after that.

He had simply vanished.

And that drove her and Dawn nuts all spring.

Tombstone Dan's company continued on, even now owning hotels, bars, and different restaurant chains. Maggie had talked with the president of the company who told her that the ownership stock in the privately held firm was in trust. He had no idea who controlled the trust and no one from the trust ever had contacted him or the board of directors. The trust just let them run the company and they were all paid well.

So by late May, Maggie had hit a dead end on her research on Tombstone Dan, although she had more than enough material about the workings of the saloons in western mining towns to fill two books, if she ever got the time to write them. Just the book on the saloons Tombstone Dan and his company had started would be fascinating reading.

Maggie had no doubt now why Dawn had found the man interesting and mysterious. He was to Maggie as well. There was no known picture of the man, but Maggie had a hunch she would have liked the guy if she could have ever met him.

Dawn came out on the deck beside Maggie and sat down.

"This is just stunning," Maggie said, indicating the pink and red caps of the tall mountain peaks spread out below them. The sunset was turning the sky bright purple and red.

"Can't believe in this year working for the Institute you have never been up here," Dawn said.

"This lodge always sounded mythical to me," Maggie said. "So not sure I wanted to see it. But now I'm glad I got over that."

"You want to explain mythical?" Dawn asked, without turning from watching the fantastic sunset.

"Just the history of this lodge makes no sense," Maggie said. "When we are back in Boise I'll show you what I mean and you can maybe make some sense out of it."

Dawn just nodded and smiled.

Maggie had no idea what that smile meant. Sometimes Dawn just did that.

Maggie had noted all kinds of strange things in her research on the valley below them, not only about this lodge, but about the beginning of the Historical Institute. So after they put the mystery of Tombstone Dan to bed, maybe doing some research on this place might just be in order as well.

And if that gave her an excuse to come back here a few times, even better.

"You excited?" Dawn asked.

"Very," Maggie said, smiling and staring as the sun turned a number of mountain tops bright pink. "And kind of scared. Not often you get to actually see a focus of historical research."

"Yeah, that is always fun," Dawn said.

Tomorrow morning, Maggie and Dawn were going to go down that harrowing road Maggie could see leading down into the valley below the lodge along a cliff face. They wanted to see if they could find the small side canyon that Tombstone Dan had bought first. Maybe that would give them a clue to what happened to him.

Dawn had been actually shocked when Maggie told her about the small side canyon. Dawn said she thought she knew everything about the Monumental Valley and hadn't known that canyon was even there.

"Here you go," Madison said at that moment, bringing Maggie and Dawn both cups of coffee. "Laced with some nice brandy guaranteed to help you sleep."

"This place is so wonderful," Maggie said, "I doubt that sleep will be the problem. I think that feather bed in my room might eat a person it is so soft and deep."

"We haven't lost a guest yet," Dawn said, sipping on her coffee with a sigh.

"I never get tired of this view, no matter how many times I see it."

"Neither do I," Madison said, taking a seat beside his wife and sipping on a mug of coffee that looked like it had some brandy in it as well.

Maggie was surprised. Only she and Dawn had driven up here today in one of the Institute's big white Cadillac SUVs.

"Great work you two," Madison said to Maggie and Dawn, "on finding that hidden canyon and that information on Tombstone Dan. I had no idea there was a hidden canyon down there off Monumental. Looking forward to seeing if we can find it."

Dawn smiled at Maggie. "He's driving that road. Hate that road. Would never drive it."

Maggie laughed. "That bad, huh?"

"It's only terrifying for about ten minutes," Dawn said, smiling.

Maggie laughed. She wasn't sure at all what she had gotten into now. This was a long, long ways from the flatlands of Wisconsin. If she didn't feel so naturally at home here, she might actually be worried.

But for some reason, she wasn't.

"Get all the guests tucked in?" Dawn asked Madison.

Madison nodded. "Crews cleaning up the kitchen and everyone is either in their rooms or out here on the deck watching this incredible sunset."

Maggie glanced around and about ten others were scattered along the long, wooden deck of the massive lodge, all facing out at the valley below watching the colors of the sunset over the mountains.

"You own this place?" Maggie asked, now even more interested in the history of the lodge.

"We are half-owners," Dawn said, smiling. "We love it up here so much, we try to live here as much as possible."

"I can see why," Maggie said. "It is the most peaceful place I have ever been. So how did you end up owning this?"

Dawn laughed. "Tell you what. We'll give you the entire sordid story tomorrow. But for now we all need rest. We're going to be leaving before the sun hits the tops of the mountains, which is very early in these mountains."

Both Madison and Dawn stood, picking up their mugs. "Enjoy the view and we'll see you in the morning. We'll stay here tomorrow night as well, so no need to pack anything but hiking clothes and sunscreen and your hat. The sun in these high mountains can really burn. We'll take care of the food and water we'll need while down there."

"Thanks for this," Maggie said.

"No, thank you," Dawn said. "I never thought I would get the chance to learn something new about that valley down there. It's exciting."

With that, the two famous historians turned and headed inside.

Maggie turned to stare back out over the mountains, their peaks now growing darker by the moment, the valleys between mountains deep pools of blackness.

What in the world had she gotten herself into? Maybe by tomorrow she would know more.

One thing she did know. After working for a winter in Boise and being at the Institute and in these mountains, she didn't want to go back to Wisconsin.

And she had a sense she wasn't going to have to.

EIGHT

Roosevelt, Idaho
May, 1909

DAN HAD JUST happened to head down to the Roosevelt general store to get supplies when he realized it was the day of the huge mudslide coming down Mule Creek.

It was the first time in a month he had been out of his home and his canyon. The spring rains this year seemed even more intense than normal and Monumental Creek was the size of a small river, angry and flowing mud beside the town. The sound of the running stream drowned out the sound of the rain on his hat.

Even the small creek in Tombstone Canyon was flowing harder than he had seen it flow in nine years, at one point, two weeks ago, causing him to rebuild his water system to his home.

At this point this year, very few people had returned to Roosevelt and he had closed up five of his six saloons and moved the bars, furniture, and pianos out last year before the snow. He knew what was coming here in May and no point in keeping those saloons going for no reason.

He had kept one saloon open for the winter, but so few people had decided to go through the winter in the valley that most days the saloon had sat empty except for the bartender. Only on the weekends when the miners at the big mine up Mule Creek got a day off did the place do any business at all.

Roosevelt was a dying town. He knew once the snow melted off the trails, some people would return to the valley, but he knew that every year now it would be less and less, especially after today.

And he was fine with that.

The boom days of Roosevelt were over. He had watched the town be born, now he was about to watch it die.

He knew that the big Monumental Lodge on the summit a few miles up the canyon above his home would stay open. He liked Dawn and Madison in the future, the couple who built it and were running it. He knew they stayed on and kept the lodge going and raised a family. But he doubted they would know him if they saw him. Chances are they had come back to the lodge before he joined the Institute. He hadn't been up there to introduce himself yet. This summer would be the time.

He spent the morning in his last remaining saloon, eating breakfast and listening to the reports from miners coming in about the slide that was headed down Mule Creek at about the speed a man could walk. It seems it had broken loose just below the big mine three miles up the steep canyon and was massive and getting bigger with every mile.

Mule Creek came into Monumental Valley right below the town, right where the valley was the narrowest.

Just as he had finished his breakfast, he heard a shout through the rain, "It's here!"

He went out into the pouring rain, making sure his slicker was tight around him and his hat down tight on his head so that no rain got down his back. Over the years he had grown used to having his pants and boots wet, but when water got inside a coat, it caused all sorts of troubles.

A group of about twenty men with shovels stood to one side of the rushing waters of Monumental Creek, looking up through the gray of the rain toward the mountain.

At first Dan couldn't understand exactly what he was seeing, then trees and rocks seemed to move and tumble like they were sticks in a stream.

The mountain he was staring at was the slide.

"Oh my god," was all he could mutter.

He was stunned at how massive it was. Completely stunned.

And it was coming directly out of what had been Mule Creek Canyon and working across Monumental Canyon.

He stood back from the group of men and now a few women, staring up through the rain at the moving mountain of mud, rock, and broken trees and brush.

It took him a while to estimate how large the slide was, finally only comparing it to the five-story Idanha Hotel in downtown Boise.

More than likely it was taller than that.

And far wider and more massive.

The rain pounded on his hat for the next hour as he just stood and watched the mountain move clear across Monumental Valley and build up against the far wall.

The sounds of trees snapping and rocks tumbling sometimes were louder than the rain.

The rushing Monumental Creek was damned up and within thirty minutes there was a small muddy lake against the side of the slide.

Dan moved back and up the side of the steep slope behind his last remaining saloon and tried to take a measure of how high above him the new mountain of rock and trees loomed.

He spent a good ten minutes looking up at the new mountain, then back down at the rain-drenched mining town.

Roosevelt was about to go under far more water than anyone could do anything about.

He knew that had happened in history, but being here to experience it was something he never could have imagined.

NINE

June 2nd, 2019
Monumental Valley, Idaho

MAGGIE WAS STILL trying to catch her breath from the harrowing ride down the side of the cliff when Madison finally pulled over and stopped.

She had been holding onto the armrest on one side and the door handle on the other the entire time.

Madison had driven the white Cadillac SUV like an expert, not too slow, but not too fast either over a road cut out of the rocks of the cliff. The road wasn't much wider than the SUV.

At times Maggie couldn't believe they could even get around corners without scraping rocks along the hillside.

On the other side of the very narrow dirt road, about ten seconds after they left the lodge parking lot, they had been thousands of feet in the air.

The sun was barely touching the tops of the mountains, so Madison needed full lights going down the cliff and Maggie, thankfully couldn't see exactly how far down it was to the valley floor. But Dawn had volunteered the fact they were at least a thousand feet in the air and Maggie's ears were going to pop a few times on the way down.

They had.

At one point Maggie had asked what happened if they met another car coming up.

"We would have to back up to a wide spot to let them go by," Dawn said, glancing back at Maggie. "Rule of mountain roads, you always back up hill."

"I'll remember that if I am ever stupid enough to drive on a road like this," Maggie said.

Both Dawn and Madison laughed.

So now they were stopped, sitting safely on the valley floor. Maggie worked to pry her fingers from the grip beside the door.

When they had come off the side of the cliff face, the road had crossed over the narrow valley floor, over a small bridge, and then turned down the valley. That was where they had stopped right in the middle of the road.

"The map shows the small hidden canyon is directly across the valley from us right here," Dawn said.

Madison nodded and pulled the SUV off the road into a small clearing and shut it off.

When the headlights went off, it was very clear just how dark this valley was at this time of the morning.

When Maggie climbed out, the cold air hit her hard.

She had already gotten used to the warm, dry summer in Boise. This was cold and very crisp and the sound of Monumental Creek was soothing.

Not even birds were chirping yet.

It was beautiful.

Wonderfully, stunningly beautiful.

"Wow," Maggie said softly, looking around.

"I love this time of the morning in this valley," Dawn said, her voice hushed as if she were in a large church.

Maggie felt exactly the same way.

Exactly.

She had on a light jacket, a sweatshirt under the jacket, and a blouse under that. Layers is how Dawn had told her to dress and Maggie was now glad she had done just that.

Maggie also had gloves and a stocking cap. She sure wasn't going to need the sunscreen for a few hours yet, at least.

"This is really something," Maggie said as Dawn and Madison closed the doors to the car with a solid thump that didn't even echo.

"This is a very special valley," Dawn said, her voice still hushed.

"Let's head back up the road and over the bridge," Madison said, putting a light pack on his shoulder and turning on his flashlight. "Easier than trying to cross the stream any other way."

He started off and Maggie dropped in behind him with Dawn following behind them along the narrow dirt road. The only sound in the still morning air was their feet against the gravel.

"Right here," Dawn said as they turned toward the creek, "is where the old pioneer pack trail started up the hillside on this side of the canyon."

Dawn aimed her flashlight at a wide area and Maggie could see the trail heading upward at a fairly steep angle.

Maggie had studied pictures of that trail and of pack trains bringing in supplies to this valley. The trail ended at the top near the lodge.

From the records, numbers of people over the years had died on that stretch of trail between here and the lodge. Maggie had no desire to try to climb that old trail at all.

"No wonder no one ever spotted this canyon," Dawn said, moving on behind Madison toward the bridge over the creek. "They were either going up or down and would have no reason to look to one side or the other on that trail. And very few people lived up Monumental past this point."

Maggie nodded and just let her nerves calm and enjoy the brisk, cold morning in the high mountains. This was going to be an adventure she would always remember.

She wanted to calm down and really enjoy it.

She had always been one to research the past. She had never gotten the chance to actually feel what the past might have really been like until now.

This valley was the past.

It was as if she had gone back in time.

They went over the bridge and the road turned up the valley, headed for that terrifying cliff drive.

The three of them stopped and Dawn took out her iPad and pulled up the map. They knew they would get no satellite service in this deep valley, but Dawn had saved the map to her device.

She brought up the scale and then overlaid a satellite image she had saved over it.

It was clear where they were standing near the bridge and it was clear the small canyon opening that Tombstone Dan had owned was about four hundred yards down the valley from them along the rock walls on the right hand side as you faced down the valley.

"Step carefully," Madison said as he shone his light ahead and eased down off the road. "No point in twisting an ankle up here."

All of them turned on the flashlights they were carrying and went back to single file, with Dawn once again bringing up the rear.

Madison worked his way through what openings in the trees and brush he could find, and the women followed as they made their way down the valley along the rock wall that towered above them in the faint morning light.

Finally, just as Maggie was about to take off her jacket because she was starting to sweat even in the cold air, Madison said, "Would you look at that?"

All three of them stopped and shone their lights ahead. From the direction they were coming, a direction no one would naturally travel along these cliff faces, they could see an opening in the rocks.

It was as if part of the cliff had simply moved about twenty feet away from another part of the cliff, opening a large crack in the wall.

"That would be impossible to see from across the valley where the trail was," Dawn said.

"No wonder we never saw it over all those years of going up and down that trail," Madison said, shaking his head.

Maggie glanced at Madison, then at Dawn, wondering exactly what Madison had meant.

Dawn saw her puzzled look and smiled. "We'll explain later over dinner, I promise."

Madison moved toward the opening in the rock.

"There was a wagon trail here," Dawn said, moving her light around to show what she was talking about. "Now covered in loose rock, but it was here."

Maggie was feeling more excited by the moment. Around them, the sun was starting to light up more of the tops of the mountains, many of which still had snow on them.

And in front of her was the opening to a small canyon that had used to be owned by someone she had worked all winter to find, Tombstone Dan.

She was experiencing real history.

Her heart was beating harder from excitement right at this moment than when they were coming down the cliff road.

She had no idea if they would find anything in this canyon left from Dan's time, but she sure was excited to find out.

And somehow, she believed they would.

TEN

Roosevelt, Idaho
May, 1909

DAN SPENT FOUR days after the mudslide had blocked the canyon helping get belongings and furniture and things from the buildings along Main Street of Roosevelt as the water backed up through the town.

Luckily, the three days after the slide the rain had stopped, leaving the skies gray and dull. Not having the rain at least made the work easier.

Very few people talked and there was no laughing at all as they all pitched in to help where they could.

The best an engineer from one of the mines could determine was that the lake would eventually stretch almost a mile up the valley floor, from wall-to-wall before the water level reached the top of the mud-slide and Monumental Creek went over it.

At the slide, the lake would be over seventy feet deep, while at the upper end it would be only a few feet deep. Two feet or seventy feet didn't matter. The town and everything a mile above it was finished.

The mountain walls were so steep on both sides of the valley that the only hope they had was to take anything anyone wanted saved a mile up the valley.

So Dan had gone home to get his packhorses and for three days all he and his horses did was make trips from the flooding lower part of the town back up the valley.

To feed people who were working, food tents had been set up by those who owned the general store above where the water would reach.

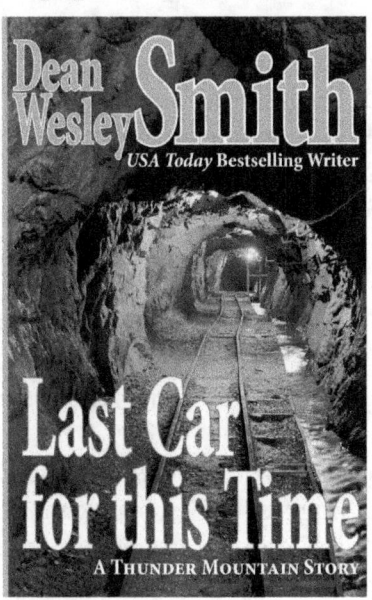

Dan's saloon manager and two others got all the furniture, poker tables, chairs, and the last piano in his last saloon hauled up the valley and stored in a massive tent. They would take it all out and down to Boise in a month or so.

Dan was very glad he had told his people in Boise last summer to shut down five of the saloons and empty them. He couldn't imagine trying to rescue everything from all six places now.

During the second day, some of the buildings on the lower side of town floated off their foundations and by the morning of the fourth day all the buildings were either floating or under muddy, dark water to the height of a tall man.

In another two weeks or so of spring run-off, the entire area would be a lake.

Some of the miners from up Mule Creek had come down and were working on building new trails up on the sides of the mountain on both sides of the lake.

And there was a new trail being built up through Mule Creek at the same time. The slide had wiped out the old one.

On the fifth day, most of the work was done. Dan took his horses back up the valley and into his hidden valley, rubbing them down and giving them some extra food for all their hard work.

Then he went up to his home sitting on the rock ledge above his hidden canyon and made himself a warm bath.

Then he cooked himself a good solid meal and took it out on his porch to eat.

Watching an entire town be born and then die in the space of nine years was something he had never expected to do. Something he had never done in all his time living in the past. It was no wonder that Dawn and Madison and Duster and Bonnie had spent so much time and energy on this mining town.

In its boom days, he had loved Roosevelt and his saloons there had made him a very rich man yet again.

But now the Monumental Valley would soon have very few people living in it, and eventually he might again be the only one. It was always going to be a special place, but this coming winter he decided he needed to spend in Boise, for the first time in five years.

He needed to be around life again after witnessing this kind of death of a dream. And Boise was about as lively a city as they came.

But first he had an entire summer to get through.

A summer of watching a valley and a town take its last gasps of life.

And he knew that when he went back to Boise, Tombstone Dan would also be dead.

It was time for him to start over once again.

ELEVEN

June 2nd, 2019
Monumental Valley, Idaho

MAGGIE FOLLOWED MADISON up the narrow canyon for about a hundred yards, her flashlight making sure the dim morning light didn't hide any wrong steps.

Then the very narrow canyon turned sharply right and after about a hundred more paces opened up into what looked like a round valley.

The morning light was enough to see the entire place.

Madison stopped and clicked off his flashlight. Maggie and Dawn joined him and did the same.

"Wow, just wow," Dawn said, looking up at the towering rock cliffs that seemed to go up into the sky around the small valley.

Maggie had seen football stadiums larger than this valley, but not as beautiful. A small stream ran from the far back wall and under some rocks beside them, more than likely joining Monumental Creek on the other side of those rock walls.

Pine trees filled the back half of the valley and a meadow about the size of a football field was directly in front of them.

But what had all of their attention was the Victorian home on a ledge above the meadow on the right side.

That wasn't possible.

How in the world did a Victorian mansion, two stories tall, get built this far up in the wilderness?

"Looks like we found where Tombstone Dan lived," Dawn said, her voice soft.

Maggie's heart was racing so hard, she couldn't even speak.

Her research had led them here. Her digging through old records and books to find the key to this wonderful place.

She was walking in history. Never in her fondest dreams had she thought that possible.

Not like this.

"How is that home here even possible?" Maggie asked.

"Tombstone Dan clearly had skills we didn't uncover," Dawn said.

Maggie agreed to that completely.

"Let's go take a look," Madison said, starting up what was clearly a wagon trail leading from the opening into the canyon up to the home.

The day around them had brightened up and Maggie just kept looking up at the beautiful Victorian home and the wide front porch overlooking the valley.

"It's got a metal roof," Madison said as they neared the flat rock ledge the home was on.

"That had to be put on in the 1930s or so," Dawn said.

Maggie agreed.

"The entire place looks to be in fantastic shape," Madison said.

Maggie had seen lots and lots of pictures of old ruins from the period this valley had boomed. None of them now, in 2019, were anything more than piles of rubble. Yet this home stood here like it could be lived in.

"Any signs of anyone living here?" Dawn asked as Madison moved along the front of the porch.

"It has been kept up," Madison said, "So more than likely at some point over the years someone lived here and kept it up since the time Tombstone Dan lived here."

He glanced back at Maggie. "Any signs Dan had children or relatives?"

"Not that I have found yet," Maggie said.

The two of them climbed up on the porch behind Madison, and Maggie turned around and looked at the small valley below them. Also, from the porch she could see the tops of the mountains to the east glowing with the morning light.

It was stunningly beautiful.

She could sit on this porch every day and never get tired of it.

Madison knocked on the ornate maple door as if someone might actually be in the home, even though they saw no signs of any life having been in the small valley lately.

The knock echoed through the hidden canyon.

Then he pushed down on the door latch and opened the large front door.

"Not locked?" Maggie asked.

"No reason for it to be locked up here," Madison said.

Inside was a front room that looked very similar to the front room in the main Institute headquarters in Boise. A massive stone fireplace filled one corner, two tall windows with drapes closed over them on both sides.

An ornate wood staircase went up just to the right of the front door.

They left the front door open and again all three of them clicked on their flashlights.

All the furniture had been covered in white sheets for protection against the dust, now looking like gray ghosts in the old room.

There was a large dining table also covered on the other side of the main room and beyond that, through a door, Maggie could see parts of what looked to be a fairly modern kitchen.

One entire wall was books, shelved neatly and covered with small cloths to protect them.

Tombstone Dan had been a reader.

Maggie felt instantly at home.

Instantly.

"No footprints in the dust," Dawn said, pointing her light at the floor.

Maggie could see the dust was pretty thick. Years thick.

"Looks like about thirty or more years of dust," Madison said, heading slowly up the stairs. "It would take that long with this tight a house for this to build up like this."

Maggie just stayed frozen in place just inside the front door, not understanding at all what she was feeling and why this place felt like home to her.

Nothing had felt like home to her before now.

Nothing.

But suddenly some empty, abandoned house in the Idaho mountains did. Strange didn't begin to describe how she was feeling.

Dawn carefully walked through the room and into the kitchen, moving slowly to not stir up too much dust.

"This was remodeled just before 1970 or so," Dawn said.

"Wasn't this entire area designated a wilderness area around that point?" Maggie asked.

"Doesn't stop people from living here," Dawn said. "No one to catch them, especially this well hidden."

"Someone spent a lot of money and time getting this place up to date and livable back about that point," Madison said, as he came back down the stairs. "Two beds covered in sheets in two rooms up there and a working toilet and bathroom. But clearly this has sat empty for a good thirty years now."

"I saw through a window what looked like a generator just outside the back door," Dawn said, coming back in the front door.

"So someone found this place before we did," Dawn said.

"A very long time ago," Madison said.

"Before we were all born," Maggie said.

Then finally, she moved carefully toward some framed dust-covered pictures on the thick wooden mantel over the fireplace.

She carefully wiped off the dust on one and with the light of her flashlight saw the smiling face of someone she guessed was Tombstone Dan. He was surprisingly more handsome than she had expected him to be.

She turned and handed the photo to Dawn. "Think that might be Tombstone Dan when he was about the age he built this place?"

Dawn and Madison both started at the image.

Both were clearly shocked.

"His name was Daniel Silver," Dawn said.

Madison nodded.

Maggie just stared at the two of them, but both Dawn and Madison just kept staring at the picture as if they had seen a ghost.

Maggie had no idea what they were talking about. And clearly at the moment both of them were so lost in thought, they weren't going to answer a question just yet.

Maggie picked up another photo and carefully dusted it off. It was of two children sitting on the front porch of this home. They looked to be around ten or so.

"Looks like there is more to discover about Tombstone Dan or Daniel Silver or whoever lived here," Maggie said.

Maggie handed the photo to Dawn and Madison.

"Oh, my," was all Dawn said. "That's not possible."

"Care to explain how you know him?" Maggie asked.

"We'll explain over dinner in the lodge," Madison said, his voice curt.

Maggie then carefully took the last framed photo off the fireplace mantel and dusted it off.

It was a portrait picture done by a Boise photograph studio from the label. It had been taken in 1934. Eighty-five years ago.

It was of Daniel Silver with gray hair, the same two children, only now both adults, and clearly a woman who had gray hair and white skin under her broad dress hat.

She had on what looked to be a frilly blue dress that fit the time. She and Daniel and their adult children looked happy. She was smiling and showing that she had freckles.

Maggie stared at her. The woman looked familiar.

Very familiar.

Maybe she was a distant relative. At this point anything was possible.

Maggie handed the picture to Dawn and Madison.

"Oh, my," Dawn said.

Then both she and Madison laughed.

"That explains things," Madison said, shaking his head.

Maggie was about to ask another question because laughing at the picture shocked her.

Madison held up his hand. "We'll have time for answers at dinner," Madison said and turned headed for the door, still carrying the picture of the family from 1934.

Maggie took one more look around the home and then followed Dawn and Madison back into the morning light on the wonderful front porch. As she stepped onto the front porch, Madison pulled the door closed tightly behind her.

Dawn sort of stopped and looked around. "So Daniel Silver, aka Tombstone Dan, lived right here. This close, and we never knew about it."

Madison nodded. "That seems to be the case. But it seems to be a different future than the Daniel Silver we knew of."

Madison indicated the framed picture in his hand and Dawn just nodded, then laughed again.

Maggie had no idea what had just happened.

Or why they were laughing.

They had found a magical-looking Victorian home in the middle of the Idaho wilderness and all it had done was bring up even more questions for her.

But clearly, for Dawn and Madison, finding the picture seemed to answer questions.

Dawn and Madison stepped off the porch and headed back down toward the mouth of the canyon.

Maggie had so many questions now she didn't know where to begin.

But that was what a good researcher did. She asked questions.

And she knew there had to be answers somewhere. And she had a hunch dinner tonight in the lodge would be a start to the answers.

At least she hoped it would.

She followed Dawn and Madison away from the old Victorian home. She didn't even need to look back because she knew, without a doubt, she would return to this little canyon.

She didn't know why or when, but she knew she would.

TWELVE

Monumental Summit, Idaho
July 17th, 1909

DAN SPENT THE next month after the flood helping where he could, but mostly just watching as the new way of life sort of settled into the valley. There was no attempt to restart Roosevelt and all trade in the valley went down the valley to Monumental City, a much smaller mining town about three miles below where Roosevelt had been.

During the peak years, Monumental Valley around Roosevelt had been full of sounds, from hammering to the piano music coming from open saloon doors.

Now Monumental Valley was mostly quiet. Dan wasn't sure if he missed the noise or not.

In the middle of July, on a nice day, he decided he needed a really good dinner, so he headed out of his hidden canyon and up the trail toward the Monumental Summit. It was time to see if Madison and Dawn recognized him from the future. He was betting they wouldn't and that would be fine with him.

The big lodge there was known for some of the best steak dinners anywhere and he felt up for one after the last few months.

He was surprised that it only took him about thirty minutes to get up there. He knew it was close, but not that close.

The lodge was as spectacular as he had been led to believe. The massive two-story log lodge looked out over Monumental Valley and seemed to fit right in with all the mountain peaks and ridgelines.

A wide, long deck ran across the face of the lodge and as he came up the trail, he could see groups of people sitting on the deck talking and laughing.

Inside, massive polished log beams gave the huge main rooms a feeling of grandness, while the stone fireplace and the warm, welcoming furniture kept it comfortable.

Madison was standing behind the big wooden desk and looked up when Dan came in.

He instantly smiled.

"A new face," Madison said. "Welcome to the Monumental Lodge."

Dan wasn't surprised that Madison didn't recognize him from the future. More than likely this Madison had come back from a time a few years before Dan joined on.

"I'm Madison Rogers," Madison said.

"Daniel Silver," Dan said, shaking Madison's hand.

Dan had already decided that for the moment he would use his real name from 2020 and this seemed as good a time as any to start using it.

"Saw you coming up the trail," Madison said. "How are things in the valley?"

"Been a rough couple months," Dan said, shaking his head. "I'm planning on sticking in the area, but not sure about how many others will be back next year. You folks going to be all right here?"

"Oh, sure," Madison said. "My wife Dawn and I like it quiet. Planning on raising a family up here, actually."

"Wonderful to hear," Dan said. "I like it quiet as well. Got a hunch we're going to get our wish fairly soon."

Madison laughed and the two of them talked for a few minutes more before Madison escorted him out to the deck to a table. "Maggie will come right by to get you a drink and your dinner order."

"Thanks," Dan said, actually feeling lighter just from one conversation. He liked to be alone, but sometimes just a little conversation could lighten a day.

He stared out over the valley beyond. The view from here was fantastic, of that there was no doubt. And as the valley calmed down and went back to its natural state, the view wouldn't have such emotion attached to it as well.

At that moment a soft voice said, "Welcome to the lodge. My name is Maggie. May I ask if you would like a before-dinner beverage?"

Dan turned and looked into the most wonderful, soft brown eyes he had ever seen. Maggie was short, with light skin, freckles, and bright red hair that was long and she had pulled back. She seemed to be a number of years younger than Dan at the moment, about his age when he first came back, and she had a smile that seemed to light up the entire deck.

In all his centuries alive he had never been so smitten on first sight by a woman.

He opened his mouth, but nothing came out, so he shut it again.

Maggie seemed to blush slightly, then said, "Madison said I was to give you the best drink on him. Something about being a possible returning customer."

Dan laughed and nodded. "I sure hope to be. I live down there, but plan on staying in my home as everyone else leaves. So yes, I will be returning. At least during the summer when the trail is open.

He held out his hand. "My name is Dan."

Maggie beamed, blushed, and then shook his hand. Her skin soft against his rough skin. "I'm Maggie."

"It is a pleasure to meet you," he said.

"The pleasure is all mine," Maggie said.

He held her hand a moment too long and she seemed slightly sad when he finally did let go.

"I would love a simple scotch whisky," he said. "And a glass of water if I may."

"And would you like to order dinner or wait a time?" she asked.

He couldn't look away from those amazing eyes. Somehow he had to learn more about this wonderful woman standing in front of him.

"Do you have some time away from your job at some point to eat?" he asked.

Suddenly he realized what he had said and what time period he was in and went on quickly. "I don't mean to be forward, but I would love to also buy you dinner, if Madison wouldn't mind. I hear the steaks here are wonderful."

Again, she blushed.

He hoped to really get used to seeing that wonderful blush that brought up her freckles and highlighted her deep brown eyes.

"The steaks are wonderful and that is very kind of you. I will get your drink and ask Madison, because I would be honored to have dinner with you."

He smiled and she blushed even more and turned away.

Five minutes later she returned without her apron over her blue dress and set his drink in front of him. She had clearly washed her face and combed back her wonderful red hair.

"I am off work now, so if your offer still stands."

He sprang to his feet and went around and pulled out a chair for her.

"Please, it would be my pleasure for you to join me," he said.

She smiled and said, "Thank you," as she sat down. "A gentleman in the middle of the mountains."

"A gentleman is a gentleman any-where," he said, smiling back at her as he retook his seat.

And for the next four wonderful hours they talked and laughed and ate and by the time the meal was over Dan knew he was in love for the very first time in his life.

And he knew he would be climbing that trail to the lodge all summer.

THIRTEEN

June 2nd, 2019
Monumental Summit, Idaho

THE RIDE BACK up the cliff face was no less terrifying, but very silent. Learning who Tombstone Dan actually was and seeing that Victorian mansion built in a hidden canyon had completely silenced Dawn and Madison.

Maggie sat in the back seat and didn't push with the hundred questions she had while at the same time trying not to look out at the thousands of feet of sheer drop going by just inches from the side of the car.

Finally, when they made it safely back to the lodge parking lot, it wasn't eleven in the morning. And they hadn't even thought of opening the food and water they had taken with them.

"Meet us in the restaurant in two hours for lunch," Dawn said. "We need to get Bonnie and Duster up here ahead of when we planned for this conversation as well."

"That bad?" Maggie asked.

Dawn shook her head and smiled. "No, just that complicated."

With that, Dawn and Madison went down the hall past the main counter.

Maggie was now very worried about what this conversation might just entail.

She started for her room, then changed her mind and turned toward the massive patio looking out over the valley they had just visited.

The view of the valley and the Idaho Wilderness stretching off as far as anyone could see was spectacular. From the deck she could see the old trail coming up the side of the hill and the valley below to the point where it turned to the left and vanished from sight.

She knew that down that valley was a small lake covering what was left of an old mining town. From pictures she had seen, some of the foundations of the buildings were still visible down through sixty or seventy feet of crystal clear water.

And at one end of the lake, where the stream had gone over the mudslide that had blocked the valley and submerged the town, a massive logjam filled part of the lake, so deep and thick and solid that you could walk across it. The logs were the remains of all the buildings that had broken apart and gotten jammed into that one area.

She wanted to see that lake because she had studied so much history of that town over the last winter. But clearly at lunch she was in for a different conversation.

A lot better than waiting until dinner as they had planned.

She ordered a glass of iced tea, a glass of water, and some nachos as a snack to hold her for the two hours.

She just sat there, munching on the nachos and sipping her tea, thinking about the impossible home she had seen this morning.

She was so buried in her thoughts that the sound of a helicopter landing just along the ridgeline almost didn't jar her.

But the voices of Madison and Duster and Bonnie coming from the main area caught her attention.

At that moment Dawn came out and got her.

"Time for lunch and some answers," Dawn said.

"I like answers," Maggie said, standing.

"You might not like some of these today," Dawn said. "But all I ask is that you trust me and Madison for the rest of the day. Listen to the entire story because it will sound totally crazy, I promise you."

Maggie just laughed. "Now I'm officially scared."

"No need," Dawn said and turned for the interior of the lodge.

They headed through the dining room and into a private back room.

Duster and Bonnie and Madison were all there, standing near a set dining table.

Bonnie was as tall as Dawn remembered her and as beautiful. Bonnie had on a silk blouse, jeans, and running shoes. She smiled and came to shake Maggie's hand.

Duster did the same.

Duster was about the same height as Bonnie and wore a western shirt, jeans, and cowboy boots.

Maggie had learned some about them this last winter in Boise. The two of them had more advanced degrees than any other couple in the world, mostly in higher math and theoretical physics. They were also extremely wealthy and known for helping others. They had built many a building and funded up many a program on University campuses around the world.

"I hear you three made some pretty amazing discoveries this morning," Duster said. "A hidden canyon off of Monumental. Just amazing. I never would have thought that possible."

"I am surprised as well," Bonnie said, indicating that they should all sit.

A large round wooden table had been sat for lunch, with glasses of water, plates, silverware and cloth napkins.

Maggie took a seat beside Dawn on her right.

Bonnie sat on Maggie's left and Madison sat next to Dawn while Duster sat next to Bonnie.

Maggie just felt out of her depth, almost like a kid at the adult's table. But she knew this lunch was because of her, and if she wanted answers, she was going to need to ask questions.

There was no more talk about the discoveries until after the waiter by the name of Steve took their drink orders and food orders.

"Please ring the bell before you come back in each time," Madison said.

Steve nodded and left.

When Steve pulled the door closed, Madison put a device in the center of the table and clicked it on. "Blocks all listening devices and recording devices."

Maggie just stared at it, wondering now even more what could be so important.

"I'm not sure where to even start," Dawn said, looking at Maggie.

So Maggie decided to give her a break with a simple question. "How did you two come to own half of this lodge? Start there."

All four of them laughed.

"Tell her the complete truth," Bonnie said to Dawn. "I am convinced she can deal with it just fine."

Maggie hoped she could live up to that faith, whatever the truth might be.

Dawn nodded and turned in her chair and looked directly at Maggie. "As I said, for the afternoon you need to trust us. We will explain everything, I promise. But at first this will sound insane."

Maggie nodded. It was already feeling insane, but she didn't say that.

"The four of us own this lodge," Dawn said. "Because in essence we built it in 1902."

Of all the answers Maggie was expecting, that wasn't even close to any of them.

She sat back in her chair and stared at the intent faces of four of the most brilliant people on the planet and wondered why they would say such a crazy thing.

FOURTEEN

Monumental Summit, Idaho
July 17th, 1909

DAN LEFT THE lodge with just over an hour of daylight left after his wonderful meal with Maggie. He didn't want to attempt that trail at night. Just far too dangerous. So even though he wanted to stay and keep talking, he forced himself to take his leave.

But he had managed to spend four wonderful hours with Maggie. She had turned out to be extremely smart and very shy, although she laughed easily.

And blushed this wonderful pink blush that brought her freckles to life on her face and neck.

During the meal and the time afterwards, she managed to keep him talking about himself, mostly, with questions that seemed to get him going about some detail or another. She clearly had a very astute and inquisitive mind that liked detail.

Since he didn't want to tell her about his previous two names just yet, and the fact that he had money, he had talked about his ten years in the Monumental Valley and how he hated that the valley was dying, but understood it.

And also welcomed it.

She seemed as guarded about her past as he was about his, but he did manage to get out of her that she was originally from the New York area, had lived in Wisconsin for a time, and had moved west last summer to Boise.

They also managed to both figure out that the other person wasn't married or ever had been married. That news thrilled him, but he hoped he didn't show it too much.

After four hours it was clear they both had secrets and he honestly was looking forward to learning hers and sharing most of his with her.

In all his years in college, then as a researcher, then back here in the past in the cattle business, and then out west, the idea of wanting to share parts of his life with another person had never crossed his mind. One simple dinner and all that had changed.

Before he had left, he had asked her if she had a day off coming up and if so, could he buy her dinner again here at the lodge.

She had agreed that in two days she was off work and that once again she would love to spend an early dinner with him.

Now all he had to do was get through the next day.

The light was getting dim as he rode into his hidden canyon and up to the stables he had built behind his wonderful home. As he brushed down Jenny and got her fed, all he could think about was the possibility that now someone might actually see this home he had worked so hard to build.

And if that someone was Maggie, he would be very, very pleased, to say the least.

He went inside, poured himself a light drink, put it on his dining room table, then went out to the small storage shed behind the house against the rocks. There he went through a secret door and into a large room. He had set up batteries charged by the moving water in the creek below his house and a computer system for writing and taking notes about this trip. It also charged other equipment.

Until he had built this home, he hadn't needed any of this, but instead just used a series of notebooks. But once the home was built and he had this secret room built, he had gone down to Boise and into the institute and back to 2020 to get

equipment, then come back to this same timeline about thirty minutes after he left.

He took his laptop and went back through his home to his dining room table. Then he opened up a new file and labeled it, "Maggie."

Then, with pleasure, he went back over his wonderful dinner, recording it every detail he could remember about it and about her.

FIFTEEN

June 2nd, 2019
Monumental Summit, Idaho

MAGGIE HAD DECIDED that her question method wasn't going to get anywhere fast, so she just asked them to start at the beginning.

It seemed the beginning was when Bonnie and Duster were working on one of their many doctorate degrees in higher mathematics, doing theoretical work on how time and matter and energy are all hooked up.

Maggie understood the basics of that. Being around a university and math professors, she had picked up some stuff.

It seemed that Duster's family had actually discovered in a mine back in the 1870s one of the not so theoretical nexus points where time, matter, and energy all came together in a physical form. While Duster and Bonnie were doing their research they came to understand what was in that old, abandoned family mine.

It seems, from what Duster said, that every time anyone makes a decision, or an event happens, a brand new timeline splits off.

Maggie understood that.

Actually, Bonnie had added, an infinite number of timelines split off because the decision is being made in an infinite number of timelines.

It was at that point that Maggie waved off the math and asked them to cut to the chase.

"Each timeline is represented in the matter side of the equation by a crystal," Bonnie said. "We figured out a way to attach to a crystal and jump into an alternate timeline and into the past of that timeline."

"We don't travel back in time in this timeline. That's not possible. But we do it in other timelines," Dawn said.

"But timelines that, for all intents and purposes, are exactly like this one," Madison said.

"Exactly," Dawn said, nodding.

"Here is the fun part," Bonnie said.

Maggie just shook her head. "There is a fun part?"

"There is," Dawn said, smiling.

"When you are in another timeline," Bonnie said, "only two minutes and fifteen seconds pass in your original timeline."

"Explain that another way as if I am actually believing all this," Maggie said.

At the moment she had no idea what she believed, but she had promised Dawn she would listen and that was what she was doing. There had to be a reason for this craziness, but so far she wasn't figuring out what that reason might be.

"Dawn and I have lived hundreds and hundreds of lifetimes in this lodge," Madison said. "From 1902 when the four of us built it onward. We have raised more kids here than I can remember their names and have died here more times than I want to think about."

"Died?" Maggie asked.

All four nodded.

"You can spend fifty years in another timeline," Bonnie said, "and die of old age and only two minutes and fifteen seconds would have passed here, in this original timeline."

"How old are you four?" Maggie asked.

All four of them shrugged.

"I counted until we got around a thousand years of living and then I stopped," Dawn said. "Counting was pointless."

Suddenly Maggie had a thought. "The reality of the details in your books?"

Dawn and Madison both nodded.

"We spend lifetimes doing the research," Dawn said, "and often write the book in an alternate timeline and bring it back with us."

"You have researched the west over the last year, correct?" Duster asked Maggie.

Maggie nodded, because at this point she doubted she could connect two thoughts into an actual sentence.

Duster stood from the table and went over to a coat rack and put on a long brown oilcloth duster and a brown cowboy hat. Then he turned around and asked, "Do I look familiar from your research?"

"Marshal Duster Kendal?" Maggie said softly.

She needed to breath slowly, very slowly.

She had seen hundreds of pictures of Duster in her research in old western towns, including Roosevelt, and thought he might be someone of interest to research.

He laughed, took off his coat and hat, and came back to the table. "Tough to avoid cameras at times."

"As if you try," Bonnie said, smiling fondly at her husband.

Silence filled the small private dining room.

Then a bell rang and Duster said, "Come on in."

And thankfully Maggie had time to stop and think as their drinks and their lunch was served.

SIXTEEN

Monumental Summit, Idaho
July 19th, 1909

BY THE TIME DAN got back up to the Monumental Lodge in the early afternoon of the 19th for his date with Maggie, his nerves were shot. He could never, in his entire life, remember being this nervous about anything before.

Thankfully, the day had turned beautiful and not too warm or windy. So he didn't even get dusty on the short ride up the trail from his home to the lodge.

He said hello to Madison and Dawn in the main entry area near the front desk. The massive log beams seemed to shine in the light through the windows and the entire place smelled of fresh bread.

He thanked them for allowing Maggie time off work to have dinner with him the other night.

"Not sure we could have kept her away," Madison said, laughing.

"She's very headstrong and very smart," Dawn said.

"I heard that," Maggie said, laughing as she came from down the hallway on the main floor behind the counter.

"Meant as a compliment," Dawn said, laughing.

Maggie looked at Dan and Dan just about melted right there in the middle of the large log room. Maggie's wonderful golden brown eyes were larger than he remembered them and her smile could melt a harsh winter.

She had on a different blue dress than the first time, this one looked like it had been designed for her. She had her long red hair pulled back off her face and tied so it went down her back.

She blushed when she looked into his eyes.

"Wonderful to see you again, Maggie," he managed to say, taking her hand and kissing it as a gentleman would.

The touch of her soft skin sent shivers along his back and he didn't want to let go.

"The pleasure is all mine," Maggie said.

"You two have a nice early dinner," Dawn said, indicating that they should head out onto the patio.

Maggie led him to the far end of the patio. "It's more private here," she said.

He held her chair for her to sit facing out over the valley and all the mountains beyond and then took his seat beside her.

"Impossible to get tired of the view," she said.

"It is," he said, looking at her.

She laughed and blushed.

And from there the next four hours were again wonderful.

He managed to find out that her passion was history and digging out the details of something in history to really understand it.

That surprised him, since his passion was also history, but he hadn't told her that yet. The business in history, from the cattle business to now the saloon business of the west.

At one point in the conversation, he decided to tell her about the fact that he had owned the six saloons in Roosevelt.

"Did you run them?" she asked.

He laughed. "No and no one but you in this entire valley even knows I owned them."

"I am flattered," she said, smiling and looking into his eyes. "I will keep your secret as if it were mine."

"Thank you," he said. "I am not sure why I kept the fact secret. I am just a person who likes to be left alone and I felt if anyone knew I was involved they would put demands on my time that I didn't want to give."

"So you didn't work the saloons and I don't assume you dug or panned for gold, correct?"

He laughed. "That is correct."

"So what did you do for the ten years in that wonderful valley down there?"

"A number of the winters I spent in Boise," he said. "But the rest of the time I worked on building a home."

"By yourself?" she asked.

"Completely," he said.

"Wow," she said, sitting back.

Then she looked at him and said simply, "You really are an amazing man."

At that point he was sure he blushed for the first time in his life.

SEVENTEEN

June 2nd, 2019
Monumental Summit, Idaho

FOR THE REST of lunch the four of them kept trying to explain things to Maggie, but at some point her brain had seemed to just shut off.

Maggie sort of remembered munching on her club sandwich. But she mostly just sort of habitually ate the fries that had come with it.

As everyone was about done eating, Dawn must have sensed that Maggie was not thinking clearly because she said to Maggie, "Let's cut off explanations until we can show you."

"Show me?" Maggie asked.

"We'll fly back to Boise and to the Institute," Dawn said.

"This all happens at the Institute?" Maggie asked. "Where?"

"Under it," Madison said.

"How many people know about this time-travel stuff," Maggie asked.

"As of this moment in 2019," Duster said, "you are the 27th person that knows."

Maggie was shocked at that number being so small. "So Ben and all the rest that work at the Institute don't know anything about this?"

"You've met a couple that do, including Director Parks, of course," Dawn said. "But otherwise, no. Almost all the researchers and librarians and staff are there to do research and will never know. That's another reason for that very strict do-not-disclose document you signed last fall. You can't tell anyone."

Maggie laughed. "I don't believe this so who would I tell that would believe me?"

"We are trusting you," Madison said.

Maggie nodded, then sat silently, not sure what to say as everyone finished the last of their lunches. Then finally a question slowly rose to the top of her muddled brain. "Why me?"

"We watch all the major researchers around the world," Dawn said. "Not only to offer grants and work space on projects at the Institute, but as possible candidates for this part of things."

"In historical researchers," Madison said, "we look for the passion and the intense focus on detail. Your work not only before you got here, but during this last year, has proven you have both the passion and the love of history and the detail focus needed to use what this offers wisely."

"Thank you," Maggie said, nodding.

"Besides," Duster said, "we like you and want you to hang around in the caves with us."

Bonnie smacked her husband on the shoulder and Dawn and Madison laughed.

"Come on," Duster said, pushing back from the table and his empty plate. "No one ever believes us until we show them, so let's go show Maggie the really fun stuff."

Dawn helped Maggie to her feet and the two of them headed out the door, through the big lobby and out the front door of the lodge.

The warm, dry air smelled of hot pine needles and felt wonderful. It cleared Maggie's head a little. Not much, but a little right now felt like a lot.

They headed across the parking lot and the main entrance road and along a wide path toward the helicopter.

Behind them Madison and Duster and Bonnie followed.

"Just trust me for another hour or so," Dawn said, "and then this will all start making a lot more sense."

Maggie nodded. "I'll do my best."

Dawn laughed. "You are doing better than most. At least you are still listening. We had one couple storm out and call us all lunatics when we tried to explain this to them. You'll meet them. They eventually came around."

"The word lunatic has crossed my mind a number of times over the last hour," Maggie said.

"I remember well," Dawn said, laughing. "Madison and I were the first to go through this. When we have some time, remind me to tell you about our first trip back into the past."

"Not good?" Maggie asked as they approached the large white helicopter.

"Eventful," Dawn said. "We camped right in the early summer of 1901, about where the front door of the lodge is now among some trees. And then lived the summer in Roosevelt in a wonderful log home."

At that moment the helicopter slowly started up and before Maggie realized it she was buckled into a seat next to Dawn.

Duster was in the front seat next to the dark-haired pilot and Madison and Bonnie sat facing Maggie and Dawn.

And a few moments later the helicopter was in the air and headed over the many mountain ranges of central Idaho toward Boise.

Maggie wished she was in the right frame of thinking to enjoy the incredible view and her first ride in a helicopter, but her mind almost felt detached.

She had no idea at all what lay ahead or what they wanted to show her to make her believe the craziness.

But these four had to have a reason to be doing this, so the best she could do was just ride along.

She most certainly couldn't let herself believe that what they were saying was possible.

That she flat couldn't do.

EIGHTEEN

Monumental Summit, Idaho
July 19th, 1909

DAN WAS DOING his best to make the afternoon and early evening last even seconds longer. He couldn't remember a dinner he had enjoyed more and conversation that kept him on his toes and interested.

As the evening went on, they both laughed more and Maggie had taken to touching him on the arm to make a point or when laughing. He loved that more than he wanted to admit.

Neither of them wanted the afternoon and evening to end, but they both knew it had to.

So to give themselves a little more time together, Maggie offered to walk Dan out to the stables to talk while he was saddling up Jenny for the ride down into the valley.

They walked side-by-side out of the door of the lodge and around toward the stables. He wanted more than anything to reach over and take her hand, but he didn't.

"This is Jenny," he told Maggie as he took his horse out of the stall and got her ready to saddle.

Maggie patted Jenny. "She's a beautiful horse. I love how the white on her chest sort of flows into the browns."

"Been with me now for eleven years," Dan said. "She and I were the ones that stumbled into Monumental Valley before things fired up down there."

"Am I too bold in saying I hope we can do this again?" Maggie asked as he put his saddle into position on Jenny while Maggie held her steady. He then worked to cinch the saddle into place.

He turned and looked at Maggie's smiling face.

"I was about to ask the same thing, but felt like I might be being a bit too bold as well."

"How about we stop worrying about being too bold with each other and just be honest?" she asked, smiling.

"I would love that," he said. "And I would most certainly love spending another afternoon with you over dinner and drinks. I can't remember when I have enjoyed a conversation as much as our last two meetings."

"And I concur," she said. "Is day after tomorrow possible? I have the afternoon and evening free."

He could feel his heart race. "That would be perfect. Tomorrow would be nicer, but the day after will be wonderful."

"Not too far for you and Jenny to come?" she asked.

He shook his head and said, "The distance doesn't matter when a wonderful companion and good meal awaits."

She laughed and his heart soared at the easy way she laughed.

"Now get going," she said. "No point risking that trail in the fading light."

She watched as he mounted up and then she turned back to the hotel.

He watched her walk away, then sighed and headed for the trail.

This had just been wonderful. And with every hour of conversation, he was falling for her more and more.

And he didn't really even know her yet.

And she didn't know him either. At some point, he wanted to tell her about his past in this timeline at least. About his money and his businesses.

And he really wanted to show her his home.

Never in his life had he wanted to open up to anyone like that before. He had always been a private person who liked to travel and live alone.

How could one beautiful, smart, red-headed woman change all that?

It worried him one moment and the next moment he welcomed it.

Mostly, he was just going to let himself enjoy his time with her and feel lucky that he had it.

NINETEEN

June 2nd, 2019
Boise, Idaho

THE HELICOPTER FLIGHT to Boise had taken just under forty minutes and the drive from the airport out Warm Springs Avenue to the Institute another fifteen.

Duster had driven with Bonnie in the front seat and Dawn and Madison and Maggie in the back.

Maggie had just given up asking any questions. Now she was just waiting to see what they wanted to show her.

The weather was almost hot for a June afternoon and Duster and Bonnie dropped them off at the front door of the Institute and then took the car around to the back.

Inside the main area of the Institute it felt cooler.

Madison went to a panel and clicked a button and a secret door slid open.

At that moment Maggie suddenly got worried. Not for her own safety, but for the slight chance they had been telling the truth.

Madison led the way into a hallway beyond that looked modern. Maggie followed and Dawn made sure the panel closed behind them.

"We'll explain all the entrances and exits later," Dawn said.

With that they went down rock staircases, clearly dug into the ground a long time ago.

Three flights down the staircases ended in a small room and Madison opened a door on the right and went through.

On the other side was a massive rock cavern with dozens of seating areas of couches and chairs. A large river-rock fireplace dominated one wall.

Against the back wall of the cavern was what looked to be a large kitchen with a massive counter and stools.

Dawn and Madison headed for the kitchen, leaving Maggie to just sort of follow and stare at the impossible cavern.

At that moment from another door, Duster and Bonnie came in and also headed to join the three of them at the kitchen counter.

"I'm making the soup," Bonnie said, going around back of the counter.

"I'll go with Maggie," Dawn said. "So make that soup hot. We're going to need it."

Maggie started to ask why soup on a warm summer day, then just changed her mind. All questions did at this point was confuse her more. They seemed to have a plan and all four knew it and clearly had done this before. So she was just going to go along until she could figure out what really was happening.

Dawn indicated that Maggie should just go with her and sort of took her arm and headed for a door off of the back of the cavern. Madison and Duster followed.

They went through a heavy metal door and then down two more flights of stairs before turning and going through another door into a massive room filled with clothing and equipment, all for different times in the past, all laid out and dated.

As they walked through that room, Maggie got even more worried. This was the kind of stuff you would need to dress right in the past.

Was this actually real?

"Don't worry," Dawn said. "We'll explain all this later as well."

They went through a door on the far side of the massive cavern full of stuff and into what looked to be a long tunnel carved out of the rock that was just lined with doors on one side.

It looked like almost a nightmare idea of a bad hotel or a jail of some sort.

Dawn walked up about ten doors and stopped and then pulled the door open.

On the other side was something that took Maggie a few moments to even see, even though lights came up just fine.

It was another long tunnel carved into the rock. Floor-to-ceiling wire mesh fence on both sides formed an aisle down the middle, with long wooden tables every ten feet or so.

The tunnel had to be half a football field long.

"Every door in the hall has a room behind it like this one," Dawn said.

It was then that Maggie noticed the glowing crystals sitting in carved pockets in the stone walls. They looked like quartz crystals, only they gave off a pink light. Five high with clipboards hanging

under each one and from what she could tell they stretched the entire length of the room on both sides.

There had to be thousands of crystals in just this one room alone.

Then she remembered what they had told her in the lodge.

"Are those timelines?" she asked, her mind wanting to shut down and just send her running back out of this nightmare.

"They are," Duster said. "All similar enough to our own timeline to be indistinguishable."

"Is this the nexus you talked about?"

"No," Duster said. "That is well protected a long ways from here. It's basically infinite in size. We brought these crystals here from near where we entered the Nexus when we built the Institute in 1880."

Maggie had no idea what to think. She was as scared as she had ever been before in her life.

Ever.

Dawn gently touched her arm. "Trust me for just a few more minutes and it will all make sense."

Maggie sort of nodded. She wasn't sure if it actually managed to be a nod or not.

Duster put on heavy gloves and opened up the fence and attached two cables to one crystal with a form of soft band. One red, one white tipped. The cables reminded her of car jumper cables and there were a lot of them curled up and stored under every table.

"Never touch a crystal," Duster said. "Extreme energy. We have never figured out what would happen if someone did actually touch one, and we honestly don't want to have it accidently happen."

He came back out of the fence and closed it, then moved over to the closest wooden table with a wooden box on one side. He attached one end of one cable to a pole on the box.

Then he adjusted a dial on the box that looked like it set a time and date.

Maggie was trembling now.

Madison picked up another heavy glove and took the remaining cable from Duster, who stepped back a few feet in front of them.

"Just put your hand on the wooden box beside mine," Dawn said.

Maggie did, surprised at the cool touch of the wood.

"See you in two minutes and fifteen seconds," Duster said, smiling.

Madison put his hand on the box next to Dawn's and then attached the other cable.

Nothing happened.

Except that Duster vanished.

No sound, no shimmering, nothing. He was there one instant and vanished the next.

"Welcome to December 17th, 1885," Madison said.

"Where did he go?" Maggie asked, indicating where Duster had been standing.

"He's still right there in 2019," Dawn said. "We are the ones that moved to another timeline, the timeline of the crystal that Duster attached the cords to."

"I'm having a hard time with all this," Maggie said.

"Come on, let me show you some things," Dawn said, taking her arm and turning her back toward the door to the long room.

"Ten minutes?" Madison asked.

"That will be perfect," Dawn said.

Dawn led Maggie out of the room and back into the hallway, then back to the staircase.

As they climbed, Maggie asked why Madison was staying behind.

"To save us this walk back down," she said. "If he unplugs the cord from the box, we end up automatically back in 2019 two minutes and fifteen seconds after we started."

"So we are going to spend ten minutes here and only be gone for two minutes?" Maggie asked, trying desperately to make some sense of all this.

"Exactly," Dawn said.

She opened the door into the large cavern. Now instead of being filled with modern furniture, there were some 1880s style chairs and couches in a group around the fireplace.

There was a solid fire going in the fireplace.

There wasn't a counter by the kitchen, but instead a large table.

"We always keep the living room area of the cavern furnished to the date," Dawn said, "Just in case someone from the outside gets down here."

She led Maggie through the same door they had come in and up the flights of stairs to same secret room behind the main room of the Institute.

Dawn pointed to a hole in the wall. "Peephole to make sure no one is out there before opening this."

Dawn looked through it and then slid the secret panel back.

The main room looked exactly as it had in 2019. Exactly. Same drapes, same furniture, everything.

Except now the room had a chill to it and there was a solid fire going in the fireplace.

Dawn moved to the front door and then looked at Maggie. "You ready?"

"Not exactly sure for what," Maggie said.

Dawn nodded. "I remember that feeling well."

Dawn pulled open the large front door to the Institute and indicated Maggie should go out.

The blast of bitingly cold air hit Maggie like a hammer.

When they had come through this door just fifteen minutes ago it had been a warm summer day.

This wasn't possible.

She went out onto the porch and Dawn joined her.

"We haven't built the stone wall yet," Dawn said. "And Warm Springs Avenue is nothing more than a wagon trail."

Maggie forced her mind to look for the details, just as she did with all her work.

Dawn was right, there were only signs of a long, wide lawn leading down through some young trees toward a wagon road. The driveway was also rutted wagon tracks.

A light snow was blowing and the cold air was cutting through Maggie's light blouse as if it wasn't there.

"December 17th, 1885," Dawn said. "Only a few years after we finished construction of the Institute." She pointed to the two Victorian mansions on either side. "We own those as well."

Maggie nodded and stepped carefully down off the porch and into the blowing snow.

She had to really feel this, to believe that what they had been telling her was possible.

Dawn had followed her into the blowing snow and looked cold, but was smiling.

"I have to ask this again," Maggie said, looking around and then at Dawn. "Why me? Why give me the chance to travel in time, or timelines, to actually live history?"

"Because you love history more than anything," Dawn said. "Just as I do, just as Madison and Duster and Bonnie do. We love it, we respect it, and we want to keep learning about it."

Maggie nodded. That was exactly how she felt and had always felt. Her passion for discovering history was completely consuming, and now she had been given a gift of being able to discover history as it happened.

"So now, one more question," Maggie said.

Dawn nodded.

"How fast can we get dry and get to that soup?"

Dawn laughed and glanced at her watch. "I would say right about now."

With that Duster appeared back in front of Maggie in the downstairs crystal room. She was standing next to Dawn and Madison, her hand on the wooden box.

And both she and Dawn were shivering so hard they could hardly stand.

Madison got between them and got them moving back for the door as Duster unhooked the crystal.

Five minutes later Maggie was standing in a warm shower and just smiling.

She had about a million questions, but now she believed Dawn and Madison and Bonnie and Duster.

Hard not to believe them after experiencing a December snowstorm in June.

TWENTY

Monumental Summit, Idaho
July 23rd, 1909

DAN WAS ONCE again excited for his and Maggie's fourth dinner. The last dinner had gone even better than the two before. He had learned a little more about her, about her passion for history.

He learned that she was about ten years younger than he was in this time-line and had spent more time in school than he had. At least in this lifetime.

He couldn't tell her about his two doc-torate degrees in business and history, one from Stanford, another from Columbia. Those were a hundred years in the future.

They talked a lot about the years he was in and around Roosevelt. Actually he talked and she seemed to always know the exact right question to get him going.

Part of the last dinner had been about the four days in May with the landslide and the flooding of the town. She was just fasci-nated that he had been there the entire time.

This dinner she greeted him with a smile and a peck on his cheek, saying she was happy he made it up the trail without a problem. They then spent the next three hours talking and enjoying a wonderful dinner on the patio.

Finally, after a rare moment of silence, Maggie said, "You said we should be bold with each other?"

He nodded.

"Then I have to say that I never imag-ined I would grow so attracted to you," she said. "I am surprised, pleased, and a little scared."

Dan felt his stomach flip at that. He had been feeling the same exact way.

"And I would like to spend a lot more time with you than we have been doing."

He agreed with that as well. And said so.

"So why surprised?" he asked.

She looked worried for an instant, then seemed to take a deep breath and decide to answer his question.

"I knew of you as Tombstone Dan before we met," she said. "I knew you liked to be alone and I expected you to be this rough mountain man instead of the handsome gentleman that you are."

He had told her his previous name in their last dinner, so that didn't sur-prise him, but it pleased him that she was happy with what she saw in him now.

"I am honored at the compliment," he said. "And that pleases you?"

She smiled. "No, being with you pleases me. I have enjoyed every minute of our time together."

"Again," he said, trying to control his smile, "I am honored and I feel the same way with you. So what worries you?"

She frowned. "That we are so differ-ent. We both have so many hidden secrets that I am afraid that revealing even a few of them might ruin what we have."

"Well," he said, "we are no different in that worry either. But I can tell you that the man you have been talking with these last four evenings is who I am and have always been."

"I do know that," she said, smiling and touching his arm. "Without a doubt. It is not your secrets that worry me, but my own."

He sat back, surprised at that. "You make your secrets sound like something I might not be able to abide with."

"That is very possible," she said. "Now I assure you, I have never done anything illegal or such things like that. It is my history that concerns me, my past."

"That troublesome?" he asked. Now he was actually worried.

She nodded. "It will not be possible for you to believe that I am who I say I am."

"I would like to be given the opportunity to try," he said, looking into those clearly worried and beautiful brown eyes.

She nodded and looked out at the fading light over the valley. "I would like to be very, very bold again."

He smiled. "I did say we should be bold with each other."

She stood and reached out and offered her hand.

He stood and took it, feeling her wonderful soft skin.

Holding his hand, she led him into the lodge and then down a hallway past the main desk.

His heart was racing and he didn't know what to say.

She opened the last door in the hallway to a large front room of a suite. He could see a bedroom beyond and a bathroom.

She led him inside and closed the door behind him. There were books on a table and a beautiful quilt of bright colors on the soft-looking bed. There was a fireplace in one corner and a window with curtains drawn.

It was very, very comfortable. As comfortable as his front room in his home.

"This is where I have been living, waiting to talk with you. I came up here to the lodge to meet you, actually."

That surprised him and he turned to look at her. "You do not work here?"

"I do not," Maggie said. "Dawn and Madison are friends of mine and they offered this wonderful suite to me so I could live here until I got the chance to meet you."

She moved over to him and pulled his head down and kissed him.

He kissed her back and it was fantastic, better than he had been imagining.

Finally she broke away, her face flushed. "Before I ask you to climb into that large claw-foot bathtub in there and scrub my back, I need to explain a little more."

He looked at the bathtub, then back at her and laughed. "Sure we can't do that the other way around?"

She kissed him again, then pushed away and said, "Sit. I have no intention of taking advantage of a handsome man all night long until he knows a little more about me."

"I have a suspicion," he said, "that I will know a lot more about you if we climb into that bathtub."

She laughed and the tension broke a little and she indicated one chair and she sat across from him on the couch.

She was so beautiful, all he could do was stare.

"I told you I am an historian, remember?"

He nodded, trying to focus on the conversation instead of the kisses and the idea of the bathtub.

"About a year ago it came to light that a man by the name of Tombstone Dan, which you have told me was your name, owned all six of the saloons in Roosevelt."

Dan nodded. "Something I had just never got around to telling you."

"I know that," she said, smiling. "I am a very good historian, a person with a passion for details."

"I have gathered that," Dan said, smiling.

"So I also know that you created the Tombstone Dan name in 1900 and filed a mining claim in a small hidden canyon just below this lodge."

"You are good," he said, nodding. "I was hoping to show you my home there when it was appropriate."

"I would love to see it," Maggie said. "Thank you. I would be honored."

Dan smiled at that and he felt his heart jump a little. That was his hope to show her his home. "It will be my pleasure."

Maggie went on. "I also learned that your real name is Dan Gray from Kansas City."

Dan again sat back, surprised. To him Dan Gray didn't really exist anymore. And it had never occurred to him to tell her about that part of his life.

Now he was a little worried.

"As I said, I am a very good historian," Maggie said, smiling.

"So why did you come up here to wait and meet me?" he asked.

"Because I found you very fascinating and I wanted, as a historian, the chance to talk with you. I did not expect you to be such a gentleman and so smart and funny and handsome."

He laughed and shook his head. He had a hunch he was blushing.

Maggie laughed. "You told me I could be bold, so I am being bold."

"So you planned to meet me, observe me, maybe talk with me," Dan said, "to satisfy nothing but an historical curiosity?"

"That describes it exactly," she said, smiling.

That sounded a lot like something he would have done as well with the right person in his field. Maggie was just ahead of her time in her research. Maybe, just maybe, if things worked out, he could talk with Bonnie and Duster and figure out a way to bring Maggie to the future.

He wasn't sure if that would be allowed, but he knew it had happened before. He just didn't remember the circumstances.

He smiled back at her. "So is there anything about me that you are still curious about?"

"Honestly, yes," she said.

He sat back. "Ask me boldly and I will tell you just as boldly."

She laughed. "I am very curious what you look like without clothes on."

Her face was bright red, almost matching her wonderful hair.

He laughed and stood and started unbuttoning his shirt.

The next moment she was in his arms kissing him again.

And in very short order she fulfilled her curiosity.

And he learned she was even more beautiful without clothes than with clothes.

PART THREE
A Problem

TWENTY-ONE

June 3rd, 2019
Boise, Idaho

FOR MAGGIE, YESTERDAY had been nothing but a dream. And today just continued it all.

Dawn jumped with Maggie a hundred years into the future of the Institute. It seemed the Institute was set up as a form of way station. The room of crystals they had gone into to jump back to December 1885 was only used for jumping from the present back.

A hundred years exactly in the future, another room was full of crystals to jump back to this time or times in between. And there were other rooms that went further forward, but that didn't concern her at the moment. Her head was full of enough stuff.

She also learned that even going into other timelines you couldn't jump back to a time when you were alive. And at all costs you needed to avoid still being in the past on the day you were born. Time would just kick you out into the nexus, which was not a place to be stuck in.

Maggie didn't understand it all, but what she did understand was that when Dawn held Maggie in a hug and jumped her forward a hundred years, Maggie was now set there, as if that was the century she had been born into.

The century of 2119.

Her anchor time as Dawn called it.

So when Maggie jumped back on her own to 2019, everything she did, even if she grew old and died, would only be two and a half minutes in that 2119 future time.

So now, if Maggie went back in time hundreds of times from 2019, spent many, many lifetimes back in the early 1900s, and then lived to old age in this present, when she died, only two and a half minutes would have passed for her aging.

And she could come back to here and do it again.

In other words, what she understood was that she was basically immortal now.

Wow, was that a hard, if not impossible thing to grasp. Dawn told her that more than likely she never would completely accept it and that dying was not pleasant, but it wasn't final for her anymore.

Maggie had no intention of trying that theory out any time soon.

So after two days, she and Dawn and Madison were sitting at the kitchen counter in the big cavern working on sandwiches. Dawn had made them all wonderful ham and cheese on fresh bread.

Combined with a glass of iced tea, it was a perfect lunch.

No one else was in the large living room area, which didn't surprise Maggie since there were so few people who even knew this existed.

"So what are you the most interested in first?" Dawn asked Maggie as they worked on the sandwiches.

"You have to ask," Madison said, laughing.

"Tombstone Dan, of course," Maggie said.

She couldn't believe she might actually get to meet the man she had been studying. This really was perfect for any historian. She could make her book about him fantastic with depth of detail and maybe even find out why he built a Victorian mansion in his hidden canyon.

And, if she was lucky, maybe even get him to show the home to her.

"Okay," Dawn said, "you are going to need a bunch of training and work before you head back to meet Dan."

"Like what?" Maggie asked. "I have the historical details down fine."

"Last time you rode a horse?" Madison asked.

"Oh, yeah, there's that?" Maggie said, laughing.

"There will be a ton of details," Dawn said. "Don't worry, you'll pick them up."

"And there is the issue of the picture," Madison said.

"What issue?" Maggie said.

Madison stood and headed around the counter to a storage area.

"In most of our past times building the lodge," Dawn said, "Daniel Silver came up for dinner regularly the summer Roosevelt went under."

Maggie nodded. "Close enough that he could do that."

"Exactly," Dawn said.

Madison came out of the storage area and handed Dawn the framed photo they had taken from Dan's home.

Dawn looked at it and slid it to Maggie.

It was clearly Dan, much older than the other picture, with two grown kids and a woman about his age with silver hair.

"Take a hard look at the woman in the picture," Dawn said.

"She looks very familiar," Maggie said.

"That's because it's a picture of you," Madison said.

Maggie actually dropped the framed photo in front of her like it had suddenly gotten hot.

Her head was spinning and she had to hold onto the edge of the counter and take deep breaths.

"In all of our previous times building the lodge and living in it and raising kids in it," Dawn said, "Dan Silver was dead. He died that same summer when his horse was spooked going down the trail and he and his horse tumbled over a thousand feet."

"So if that's the case," Maggie said, "How can that be me in the photo with him?"

"You clearly go back and somehow stop him from making that fall," Dawn said.

"Nice looking kids," Madison said, looking at the picture. "I bet your great-great grand-kids are about your age now."

Maggie actually shuddered at that sentence. Not that she didn't like kids, but the idea she had great-great-grand-kids her age now was more than she wanted to think about.

Far, far more.

"Something to research," Dawn said, smiling at Maggie.

Maggie just stared at the picture, not knowing what to think.

None of this was even possible, yet they were right, that was her in that 1934 photo.

An older version of herself.

Now what was she going to do?

TWENTY-TWO

Monumental Summit, Idaho
July 26th, 1909

DAN SPENT THE next three wonderful days and nights with Maggie in the lodge. They mostly never left her suite except to go out onto the deck for dinner and to watch the spectacular sunsets.

Each morning Maggie had gone out and brought them back breakfast.

The two of them just fit together in so many ways. Never, in all his life had he imagined being with a woman like her. She made him laugh, he made her laugh, and as each wonderful day went past, he didn't want to leave her side.

He felt like he was really getting to know her and she clearly knew all of his secrets but the one fact that he was actually from 2020. And that was easy to hide since it would be impossible for Maggie to believe anyway.

But he still felt at times, like there was a shadow going by on her face, that she had one more secret as well. But he now trusted her to tell him when the time was right.

And whatever the secret, he wasn't worried at all that it would affect how he was feeling for her.

So as the days went by, she asked him if he would not only show her his home, but take her down to the lake and tell her firsthand what had happened.

He had gladly agreed to do both.

He couldn't believe that the summer that had started off with so much destruction had turned out so wonderfully for him.

That evening, he and Maggie had dinner with Madison and Dawn. At first he had felt a little nervous about staying with Maggie in her room, but Madison and Dawn were completely comfortable with it. And clearly considered Dan and Maggie a couple.

And neither Madison nor Dawn seemed to have the slightest idea that he was a historian from the future, even though he had used his real name. Clearly this Madison and Dawn had left to come back before he joined the program.

And that evening Madison and Dawn had news. Dawn was pregnant with their first child.

And that made the entire meal a party and a celebration.

After that meal, Dan felt like Dawn and Madison were friends. And might be lifelong friends. When he got back, he would go talk with them in 1920.

When he and Maggie got back to her suite, she kissed him long and hard and then looked right into his eyes. "Did you ever think about having children?"

"Honestly, no," he said. "But until meeting you I never thought I would find someone to want to be with to have kids. How about you?"

"The exact same answer," she said. "I had never thought of it because I figured my work and passion for history would never allow me to get close to anyone."

He laughed. "Well, glad I turned out to be such a good history project."

She smiled and said, "You have no idea."

And then she kissed him again and one thing led to another for a number of hours that night.

TWENTY-THREE

July 1st, 2019
Boise, Idaho

FOR MAGGIE, THE last month had been tough and tiring. She got training in riding, firing a rifle, cooking over a campfire, digging a latrine, and other things a woman needed to know how to do in the west in 1909.

The plan had turned out fairly simple. Dawn and Madison and Bonnie and Duster were going to go back to 1900 as they always did when they wanted to build the Monumental Lodge in a new timeline.

They always built it exactly the same, from timeline to timeline.

Then Duster and Bonnie planned on going their own ways and Dawn and Madison planned on living in the lodge and raising another family. For some reason, not even understood by the mathematics, when Dawn and Madison had kids in different timelines, the kids were always different.

And Dawn and Madison really loved living in the lodge and raising a family. Maggie honestly had no idea what that would be like, but listening to them talk about some of their hundreds of families they had raised and the lifetimes they had lived, she felt envious.

Maggie's goal for this first trip back was to get used to living in the west, meet Dan, and with luck get some research done and more information about him for her book.

She put out of her mind that picture of him and her and their kids. That was a path she didn't want to think about at all.

However, she did worry about him dying on that trail. A nagging worry that wouldn't leave her.

The day they were all ready to go, Maggie found it interesting how they hooked up the crystal.

They were all going back to the same timeline, and they would all be gone for just two minutes and fifteen seconds. But they didn't want to be tied together in case one wanted to leave the timeline early.

So Dawn and Madison had one wooden box machine hooked up to the crystal and set for June 1900. Bonnie had one machine and Duster had another machine hooked up to the same crystal, both set for May of 1898.

Maggie had a fourth wooden box machine hooked to the same crystal, only hers was set for early June 1909. Madison would meet her and they would go up to the lodge together.

That way all of them could spend their varied times in the past of that timeline yet all return to the Institute in just over two minutes.

Maggie was so excited and so scared, she almost couldn't stand still.

So with all the boxes hooked up, Dawn said, "On the count of three, place your hand on your machine."

She counted to three and Maggie put her palm flat on the box in front of her.

Nothing.

Except that the other four vanished.

She stepped away from the machine, trying to catch her breath. Was she really in 1909?

Was all this really possible?

She was at the same time scared out of her mind and excited. And she couldn't tell which emotion was which.

She turned and headed back out of the crystal room and through the supply area and upstairs to the living room. The supply area clearly only had stuff for 1909 and earlier, so she had made it.

Madison was stretched out on a couch in front of a low-burning fire in the fireplace. The couch was an early 1900s style and the kitchen counter was still just a large dining table.

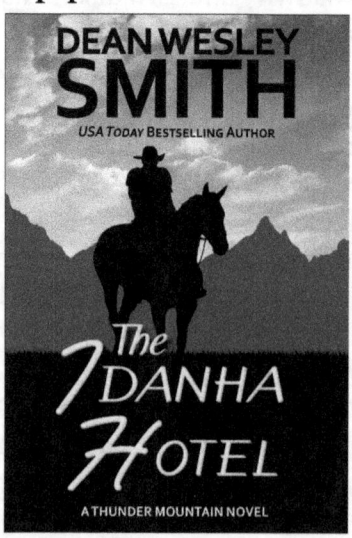
No one else was in the big cavern.

She let the door close behind her loudly, then said, "I think I made it."

Madison stirred and looked up and smiled. "Great to see you again."

Right at that moment Maggie realized that even though she had seen Madison just a minute before, he and Dawn had lived nine years since that moment. And Bonnie and Duster had lived even longer.

This jumping in time was going to take some getting used to, of that she had no doubt.

Since she had arrived early in the morning, and Madison had everything ready to go, within an hour they were headed out of Boise and up toward Monumental Summit.

It took them two days and on the second day she had to do some walking. But when they finally reached the lodge, Maggie had never felt so good.

She was actually living and surviving in the history that she had studied for so long. The feeling was like a perfect dream she didn't have to wake up from.

She loved the suite they gave her on the main floor and clear to the back. The high mountain air and the fantastic feather bed gave her the best nights of sleep she had ever had.

So she felt ready by the time the moment came when Madison knocked on her door where she was reading and said, "Dan is coming up the trail."

Ready and so excited, she felt like a young girl meeting a rock star. She knew so much about Tombstone Dan, she might as well have had a poster of him on the wall of her bedroom.

To her he was a rock star.

She watched from down the hall as Dan came in and introduced himself and Madison had him go out and sit on the patio.

Dawn motioned for Maggie to come out and handed her an apron. "Ever waited tables before?"

"In undergrad the first year," Maggie said, looking at the apron like it was an alien.

Dawn laughed and took the apron and tied it over Maggie's blue dress.

"You wanted to meet Tombstone Dan," Dawn said. "What better way than to serve him drinks and dinner."

Madison just laughed as Dawn pushed Maggie toward the front deck.

Maggie was convinced right at that moment that in high school going to her first prom she hadn't felt this stupid or afraid.

She just hoped she didn't drop something on Tombstone Dan.

TWENTY-FOUR

Monumental Summit, Idaho
July 28th, 1909

THE NEXT DAY IT rained, so they decided to wait a day until it cleared before going down the trail to show Maggie his home and then go down to the lake where Roosevelt had been.

They spent the day in her room, mostly just reading. He found it wonderful that she loved to read and didn't mind that he read a lot as well. In fact, they both agreed that their best idea of a perfect evening was a hot cup of tea or cocoa, a nice fire, a comfortable quilt, and a good book.

So, as the following day broke clear, with just a little haze covering the ground, they got ready to go.

Dan had washed the two shirts he had brought with him twice, and he suggested that if they spent too long at the lake, they could stay the night at his place, so Maggie should bring her things.

Maggie had just laughed and said, "Already packed. You said you liked bold, remember."

He just laughed and kissed her.

So they said goodbye to Dawn and Madison and headed down the trail.

Dan didn't think much about the trail, but Maggie seemed deathly afraid of it, something he would not have expected from her.

She started off confident, but within a hundred yards of the top, it seemed that all she wanted to do was get off her horse and hold on tight to the rocks.

"Do you ever get used to this?" she asked Dan who was riding ahead of her.

"I just don't look down," he said, smiling back at her. "Just let your horse have some play in the reins and focus on my horse's ass."

"I would rather focus on yours," she said.

He laughed again, then said, "That would work as well."

They rode in silence for a few more seconds, then she said, "Surprisingly, it helps."

Dan laughed.

It was right at that moment that Jenny jerked under him and reared up and started backwards.

Dan caught a glimpse of a large rattlesnake in the middle of the trail ahead of them.

He patted Jenny to try to calm her, but the snake moved again and Jenny went back again and spooked Maggie's horse as well.

Both horses lost their footing.

"Jump to the trail," Dan yelled.

He could see that Maggie tried to dive off toward the uphill side of the trail, only to fail as her horse slipped and scrambled over the edge, pulling her with it.

Jenny went over as well, slipping and scrambling in the loose rock, pulling Dan with her.

That was the most terrifying moment Dan had ever lived as he fell with Jenny toward the valley floor a thousand feet below.

Maggie had already tumbled once under her horse on the steep slope.

Then his head hit something and everything went black.

And he found himself back in one of the long rooms full of crystals in October 17th, 2020.

That entire life, as normal, had only taken just over two minutes.

The wooden tables stretched down the middle of the crystal room. He was at the one farthest from the door. The wire fence on both sides of the narrow cavern made it feel even tighter and the glow from the crystals gave it an eerie look.

"Damn it all to hell!" he shouted, banging his hand on the wooden table. "Just damn it!"

He banged his hand on the wooden table a few more times.

The sound echoed for a moment and then again the room went silent.

The image of Maggie going over that edge played over and over. How could he have lost her so quickly, so stupidly?

He stood there, leaning on the table, trying to catch his breath. He just wanted to break something.

Maggie's wonderful face just filled his vision, her smile, her laugh, how he felt with her.

He had fallen in love with a woman for the first time in his life and then lost her after only a very short few days.

He had watched her fall to her death.

Finally, he stood up straight and took a couple deep breaths.

He had to think.

"Think, stupid, think!" he said to himself as he paced up and down in the big room.

He had options.

He had lived for a very long time in the past. He knew what was possible and what wasn't.

He could go back.

But if he wanted to meet Maggie again, he would have to live the life she researched once again right from the start.

And he had to do it the exact same way. Every detail.

There was no telling what detail he had done that had caught her attention and brought her to that lodge to meet him.

Could he do that?

He paced and thought about it.

Yes. He could do that.

Luckily, when he came back to get the computer equipment, he had stored his diaries from all his early years here in 2020. He had them to help him not miss a detail.

And this next time he would create his home even nicer because he had already built it once and now had even more skills.

He put on heavy gloves and unhooked the cords from the wooden box first. Then he went in behind the wire mesh screen. He unhooked the cords from the crystal.

Then he marked on the clipboard under the crystal the dates, his name, and everything needed for another traveler to know.

Then he moved the cords to the crystal right below the one he had just lost his life in.

Then he went out of the door to get his notebooks from his locker.

He was back with them in a leather pack in ten minutes.

With the heavy gloves on, he again hooked the cords to the wooden box and set the date for the exact time and place he had jumped back to before.

Then he took off the gloves and touched the wooden box.

The life of Dan Gray aka Tombstone Dan had just started all over again.

It would take him almost fourteen years, but he would again meet Maggie if he did this all correctly.

For Maggie, he would do it.

She was worth it.

TWENTY-FIVE

July 1st, 2019
Boise, Idaho

ONE MOMENT MAGGIE was staring at the back of Dan while trying not to be so terrified of the steep trail and the next thing she knew she was standing in the crystal room with her hand on the wooden box.

Jenny, Dan's horse had reared, going back into her horse, and both she and Dan and their two horses had gone over the edge of that narrow trail.

It was horrifying and then everything had gone black. She must have hit her head almost instantly.

Madison and Dawn and Duster and Bonnie were standing in the crystal room.

Bonnie turned to Duster and hugged and kissed him. "I missed you big guy."

"I missed you as well," Duster said.

Maggie shook her head. This couldn't be real.

She had just made love to Dan last night, kissed him a few minutes ago in 1909.

Dawn instantly jumped to Maggie.

Suddenly Maggie realized she had died on that trail and was now alive.

She had died, so she had ended up here.

Dan was dead as well, as he had done in all the earlier timelines that Dawn and Madison remembered.

Dan was dead.

The idea of that sort of sunk in.

And with that thought Maggie broke into sobs in Dawn's arms.

She had fallen in love with a wonderful man and then lost him, all in the space of a few weeks a hundred years in the past.

And two minutes and fifteen seconds of the present.

How was that even possible?

"What happened?" Bonnie asked as Duster went about marking on a clipboard under the crystal as being used and by who and the dates.

"She and Dan died on the trail from the lodge down into the valley," Dawn said. "A few weeks after they met."

"Snake," Maggie managed to say. "Spooked Dan's horse and mine as well."

"We know," Dawn said, softy, hugging Maggie. "A dozen people saw it happen from the lodge balcony. I am so sorry."

"We buried both you and Dan above his house in his hidden canyon," Madison said.

Maggie couldn't grasp the concept of being buried next to Dan.

Or being buried at all for that matter.

"There was another gravestone there as well," Dawn said. "For the next forty years we kept up Dan's house. We bought Dan's company, including the house and one of our kids ended up living there with his wife and kids."

Maggie looked at Dawn. "How many years were you there after I died?"

Madison laughed.

Dawn smiled. "I made it until 1946. Madison broke a hip and caught pneumonia and died in 1940. So over thirty more years."

"How long was your trip?" Maggie asked Bonnie.

She needed to think about something besides that image of her and Dan going over that edge.

"I died in San Francisco in 1947," Bonnie said, smiling. "I had some wonderful years."

"Died in a hospital in Denver in 1941," Duster said. "Nasty case of pneumonia as well, if I heard what the doctors were saying through my fever. I can tell you, if I was a writer, I would have some great stories of poker games."

"So we all died?" Maggie asked.

Duster nodded as he and Bonnie headed for the door, arm in arm. "Sometimes these trips work that way."

"And sometimes you come back and pull the wire," Dawn said, turning Maggie toward the door behind Duster and Bonnie.

"And all those years of living and those few weeks I did only took a little over two minutes here?" Maggie asked.

"See why we can get the detail in our books?" Madison asked as he closed the door behind them.

Maggie could see that, but there was one thing she didn't understand.

"What about the picture of me and Dan and the adult children? How can that happen?"

Duster looked over his shoulder and smiled as he and Bonnie reached the supply room. "You got to go back, meet him again, and make damn sure the two of you don't die on that trail the next time."

Dawn nodded. "Dan is still alive in his time, just as you are still alive in your time."

"And now that you know how to meet him," Madison said, "you can plan better for the next time."

All Maggie could hear were the two words "next time."

If that picture was going to happen, there had to be a next time.

And she desperately wanted there to be. Desperately.

PART FOUR
A Solution and Another Problem

TWENTY-SIX

July 3rd, 2019
Boise, Idaho

FOR TWO DAYS after getting back, Maggie spent time between her office in the big Institute library building in the downtown area and in her condo. The Boise summer days were warm, the evenings cool. No humidity, which she remembered sweating through with a Wisconsin summer.

Two evenings in a row she had sat on her patio and watched as the rafters drifted past on the Boise River, just enjoying life and the wonderful evenings. She found herself more than once wishing that Dan was sitting her beside her. She had a suspicion that he would love it.

Even though her condo had a modern kitchen, the most modern bed, and a bathroom that had everything, including a swirl tub, she missed her room in the lodge.

But she had to admit, most of all she missed Dan.

Never in her wildest thinking had she ever expected to fall in love like she had fallen for Dan, and then miss him so much after only knowing him for a short time.

That didn't seem like her at all, yet she felt fine with it.

As the two days went on, she slowly developed a plan.

First off, she was going to have to go and meet Dan again and not be too forward, or bold, as he put it, to scare him off. That was going to be both difficult and fun.

Then she needed to save him from ever falling off that trail. So her idea was simply this. She needed to ask him a favor and that favor was that he never rode down that trail, but instead walked.

Walking wouldn't take much longer and if they had been walking, they both would have still been alive and together.

She would ask him to do it as a favor for her, nothing more.

Then the second part of her plan was more complex. And that was where she needed to talk with Dawn and Madison.

So on the morning of the third day back, she asked to meet Dawn and Madison in the living room area under the Institute.

Both of them were dressed as normal in comfortable shirts, jeans, and running shoes, the same clothes that Maggie had on.

When she got there they had two calendars of the year spread out on the bar and two appointment books. They were going through their speaking engagements and travel plans, comparing notes. Since both of them were respected historians, they were in high demand and even though they didn't need the money, they both felt it was part of what they did to attract new interest in the study of history.

Maggie went around the counter to the fridge and got herself a bottle of water. She had walked down the river trail to the Institute and even though it was only nine in the morning, the summer air was dry and heating up.

She had to admit she loved the summers in the west far more than the summers in Wisconsin. It cooled down at night, just like it did in the mountains.

When Dawn and Madison got to a break point, they both closed up their calendars and books and sat back. Maggie stayed on the kitchen side of the counter so she could face them.

"You about ready to go give it another try with Dan?" Dawn asked.

"Almost," Maggie said.

She told them the first two parts of her plan and Madison laughed. "We never ride up that trail. And after your and Dan's accident, we told all guests to walk down the trail. No one ever died on that trail by walking it."

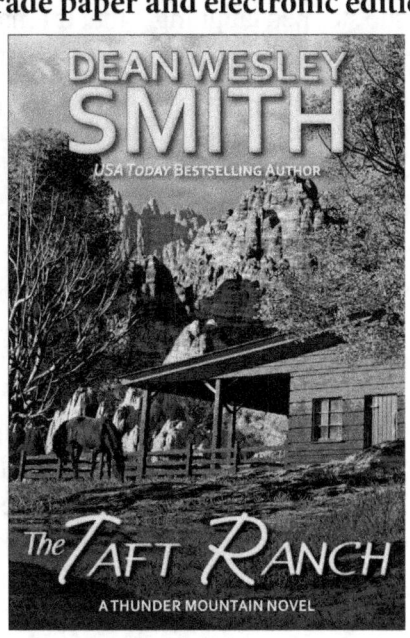

"Good to hear," Maggie said, grinning.

"So why did you need to talk with us?" Dawn asked.

"Well, first, to ask if you were interested in going back and building the lodge again and all that effort."

Both of them laughed at that. "We love doing that and living there," Madison said.

"More than you can ever realize," Dawn said. She patted the books and schedules. "We love it here and all of this as well. But those lifetimes in that lodge, those children, that is who we are."

Maggie just shook her head. "I would be so afraid to have a child back in those days, with medicine of the time."

Dawn once again laughed. "Oh, trust me, I have a modern doctor and we have modern equipment in that lodge at all my births. I'll explain how that works at some point."

"And being able to know you won't actually die helps some as well," Madison said.

"That and good drugs," Dawn said, winking at Maggie.

"So I was wondering," Maggie said, after she stopped laughing, "that if I manage to get Dan to fall in love with me again…"

"You will," Dawn said.

Maggie sure hoped so. She went on. "And if we make it down that trail alive and eventually decide to get married and have kids and create that picture we found from 1934, what is the chance that Dan might be brought forward if I still love him after all that and he still loves me?"

Dawn and Madison looked at each other. Then Dawn turned back to Maggie. "Why don't you first get through all those ifs and then after you have lived for decades and died of old age with Dan, see how you feel?"

Madison nodded.

"So it's possible?" Maggie asked.

"We have figured out that anything is possible when it comes to timelines," Dawn said. "Desired is another matter."

"Thank you," Maggie said, smiling. "That's all I needed. When would you like to go build another lodge? Tombstone Dan ain't getting any younger, you know."

Dawn and Madison both laughed and after a quick phone call to Duster and Bonnie, they decided to go in the morning.

TWENTY-SEVEN

Monumental Summit, Idaho
July 17th, 1909

DAN STARED OUT over the valley in front of the lodge. The view from here was fantastic, of that there was no doubt. Better than he had remembered it, actually.

The last two months had been difficult, at best. Watching Roosevelt as a town he had loved die in front of his eyes had been as hard the second time as it had been the first.

But the last few months of waiting for Maggie to be up in the lodge had been even harder.

After fourteen years, he had done everything exactly the same except for adding in even more craftsmanship in his home.

Dan felt his stomach twist just looking down into Monumental Valley. But he knew that as the valley calmed down and went back to its natural state, the view wouldn't have such emotion attached to it as well. And this time he hoped he and Maggie would survive to see it.

If he had done enough right over the years to get her back here.

At that moment a soft voice said, "Welcome to the lodge. My name is Maggie. May I ask if you would like a before-dinner beverage?"

Dan turned and looked into the most wonderful, soft brown eyes he had ever seen.

She was even more beautiful than he had remembered over the last fourteen years. She was shorter than he remembered, but with the same light skin, freckles, and bright red hair that was long and that she had pulled back.

And her smile seemed to light up the entire deck.

He damned near choked he was so nervous. He couldn't believe he had made it here, this far, this many years.

He had done it all correctly again. She had come back.

She also looked a little nervous, more than he remembered her being last time.

He felt completely nervous as well.

He opened his mouth, but nothing came out, so he shut it again.

Maggie seemed to blush slightly, then smiled and said, "Madison told me I was to give you the best drink on him. Something about being a possible returning customer."

Dan laughed, remembering that she had said that last time, and nodded. "I sure hope to be. I live down there."

He pointed to the valley below. "But I plan on staying in my home as everyone else leaves the valley. So yes, I will be returning."

He held out his hand, which surprisingly and thankfully wasn't shaking. "My name is Dan."

Maggie beamed, blushed, and then shook his hand.

Her skin soft against his rough skin.

Wonderful.

"I'm Maggie."

"It is a pleasure to meet you," he said.

He did not add the word *again*.

"The pleasure is all mine," Maggie said.

He held her hand a moment too long and she seemed slightly sad when he finally did let go.

But a little less nervous.

He felt less nervous as well. He was on script.

"I would love a simple scotch whisky," he said. "And a glass of water if I may."

"And would you like to order dinner yet?" she asked.

He couldn't look away from those amazing eyes. He found it surprising that he had been so bold the first time and had asked her to join him, but this time he most certainly wanted her beside him as soon as possible.

"Do you have some time away from your job at some point to eat?" he asked, remembering his lines from all those years earlier.

Then, as he had done the first time, he went on quickly. "I don't mean to be forward, but I would love to also buy you dinner, if Madison wouldn't mind. I hear the steaks here are wonderful."

Again, she blushed and sighed. "They are wonderful and that is very kind of you. I will get your drink and ask Madison, because I would be honored to have dinner with you."

He smiled and she blushed and turned away.

Five minutes later she returned without her apron over her blue dress and set his drink in front of him. She was smiling a very large smile, but the nervousness seemed to have returned a little.

"I am off work now, so if your offer still stands."

He sprang to his feet and went around and pulled out a chair for her.

"Please, it would be my pleasure for you to join me," he said.

She smiled and said, "Thank you," as she sat down. "A gentleman in the middle of the mountains."

"A gentleman is a gentleman any-where," he said, smiling back at her as he retook his seat.

He was amazed he remembered that line as well.

Then, for the next four wonderful hours, they talked and laughed and ate just as they had done fourteen years ear-lier for him.

By the time the meal was over, Dan knew he was in love and all the work to repeat this lifetime had been worth it for this one dinner.

Now he needed to work to stay alive and extend the time with her.

And this time actually get to show her his home.

TWENTY-EIGHT

Monumental Summit, Idaho
July 28th, 1909

MAGGIE STOOD ON the wide deck and watched and worried as Dan rode away from their first meeting and down the trail. The memory of them tum-bling over that trail edge still sent shiv-ers down her back and woke her up most every night. And it made sense that it would since in real time for her it had only been seven days ago that it had happened.

Seven days ago she had died.

But she was alive, standing here, and Dan was alive. And they had had a sec-ond wonderful "first dinner" together.

When he finally vanished from sight, she took a deep breath, turned and went back into the lodge.

The smile on her face was so wide, it felt like it was trying to crack the sides of her mouth.

"How'd it go?" Dawn asked, laugh-ing as she looked up and saw Maggie come inside.

"I managed to stay on the same script from the first time and not just tear off his clothes and jump him right there."

"Ah, willpower," Dawn said, laughing.

"Difficult. Damned difficult."

They chatted for a few minutes, then Maggie went back to her suite and pulled out her notebook and started to go over the lines she remembered from their second date.

She was going to do her best to keep everything on script, right down to the moment she said she wanted to see him naked.

And she did.

The second time through she real-ized she loved him even more, which she found even more amazing.

So finally, on the morning of the day they were to head down the trail to see his home and then go on to visit the lake that had covered Roosevelt, she turned to him.

"I have a bold and very, very serious favor to ask of you and I know it will make no sense."

They were both still in bed, still naked, and had just been talking about a book he had been reading.

He looked under the covers and then shook his head, "I don't have any more clothes to take off."

She laughed and kissed him, then looked him right in the eye. "I need you to promise me you will only walk that trail from the valley floor up here to the lodge from now on out."

He looked very puzzled, a look she hadn't seen on his face quite like that before.

"Dawn and Madison have said they are telling people headed into the valley to do that now. They have convinced me it is a good idea and asked me to talk with you. It isn't that far and leading a horse is the safe way."

"So why is this so serious?" he asked.

She could feel the emotion of waking up in the cavern after they both had died and she tried to hold it back, but couldn't completely.

"I am falling in love with you," she said. "And I don't want to lose you."

He hugged her and then kissed her.

"I don't plan on going anywhere," he said.

She nodded. "I know this land is dangerous, but you understand me and my passion for research and detail. And I did my research on that trail out there and except for people who tried to climb the trail in bad weather or at night, everyone who died on that trail died because they were riding a horse. No one has died walking it. So would you please promise me on that one mile stretch to walk it?"

"If it means that much to you," he said, "I will walk it."

"Thank you," she said, going into his arms and kissing him with as much passion as she had ever had.

An hour later they were both lying there, breathing hard. The quilt had long before ended up in a pile on the floor.

"You know," he said, "you can ask me favors like that any time you want."

She rolled toward him and smiled. "I can?"

He looked into her eyes and then said, "Absolutely. But you have to do me a favor in return."

"What's that?" she asked.

"Wait a few hours between each one."

She laughed and kissed him and knew, right there, that she was going to love spending the rest of this life with this wonderful man.

TWENTY-NINE

Monumental Summit, Idaho
July 28th, 1909

DAN LED HIS horse, Jenny, down the trail away from the Monumental Lodge, just as he promised Maggie he would do.

And just as he had planned on doing anyway. In fact, every time he had ridden away from the lodge on Jenny, he had dismounted and walked the rest of the way as soon as he got out of sight of the lodge.

Maggie was leading her horse a pretty good short distance back. They had talked about her not getting too close to him on the trail.

She was dressed as a woman of wealth would dress, with riding slacks, a silk blouse, a warm jacket over the blouse, a wide hat, and leather gloves. Dan had never thought to ask Maggie where she got her money or that much about her family. After seeing her riding clothes today, he made a note to ask her at some point.

The sun was just clearing the tops of the mountains to the east and the air still had a bite to it, although it promised to be a warm summer day. The ground was still a little damp from the rain yesterday, but not bad and not enough to make the rocky trail even the slightest bit slick.

The thousand feet to the valley floor below the trail was shaded in shadows and made him feel like he was walking along the edge of a black pool.

They had only gone a few hundred yards, the lodge was still dominating the skyline behind them, when suddenly Jenny yanked back on her reins.

Dan automatically stepped back with her, working to keep her calm and on the middle of the narrow trail.

Maggie had stopped about five horse-lengths back, her eyes wide.

Dan glanced ahead and there on the trail was a rattlesnake. If he had taken another four steps he would have kicked it, it blended in so well with the ground color.

What in the world was it doing out so early? And up this high? He had wondered that for fourteen years. Rattlesnakes were usually found in the rocks down near water along the major creeks and rivers. Whatever the reason, the snake was now curled in the middle of the trail and its rattle was going hard. He and Jenny had clearly startled it.

Dan let Jenny just back up a few more feet, calming her as she went, focusing on her, making sure she stayed solidly in the middle of the trail.

When they reached a point that Jenny felt calmer, Dan picked up a medium-sized rock and tossed it at the snake.

The rock hit the snake solidly and the snake moved quickly over the edge of the trail and down into some larger rocks ten feet below the trail. Dan watched until it disappeared from sight.

"You two all right?" Maggie asked.

Dan patted Jenny. "We're fine. Jenny here just has never liked snakes."

"Do you blame her?" Maggie asked.

Dan laughed and glanced back at where the snake had been. With luck they would make it past this point this timeline.

Dan didn't allow himself to look down, but instead patted Jenny one more time and said, "Ready to go girl?"

"You talking to her or me?" Maggie said, smiling. "You know I'm always ready."

Dan just laughed and then carefully led Jenny forward, past where the snake had been and on down the trail.

Twenty minutes later they reached the bottom in the cool shadows of the valley floor. Dan led Jenny over to the clear Monumental Creek water and let her drink.

Maggie joined him and let her horse drink as well.

"Really glad I was walking that," she said. "That trail is terrifying on foot. My heart never would have survived being on a horse."

"It was a good idea," he said, going and kissing her. "Thank you for asking me to do that."

"Oh, if I remember right, it was my pleasure," Maggie said, smiling.

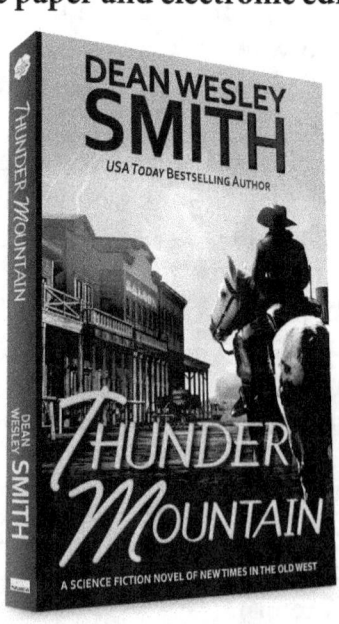

He laughed and they both got a cold drink of crystal clear water from the stream. The air still had a sharp bite to it in the shadows, but Dan knew that in his canyon it would be warmer, since the sun hit there sooner than in the main Monumental Canyon.

And he was really excited to show Maggie his home.

He built it the first time never expecting anyone to see it. He had built it for himself, by himself.

This time around he had still built it himself, but he had built it with showing Maggie in mind.

And that had made him take even more care with the details.

Now he really hoped she would love it as much as he did.

THIRTY

Monumental Valley, Idaho
July 28th, 1909

MAGGIE RODE BEHIND Dan as they crossed over Monumental Creek and through some trees. She remembered how hard it had been for them to go through this brush when Madison and Dawn and she had first come here over a hundred years in the future.

The brush wasn't much thinner now and there really wasn't much of a trail. But Dan seemed to find the holes in the brush just fine and fairly quickly they were at the rock wall where the hidden canyon started.

"How in the world did you ever find this?" Maggie asked, one of the many questions she had wanted to ask him when the time was right.

"I was over near where we watered the horses," Dan said, "and caught a glimpse of this crack through the trees. As a cattleman in rock canyon country, hidden canyons are how you lose a lot of herd, so I got trained to just sort of see them."

"Makes sense," she said, following Dan along the wagon-sized trail into the canyon. Between the towering rock walls, it felt almost like night, even though the sun was lighting up all the upper slopes on the mountains around them.

In short order the canyon turned to the right and then pretty soon it opened up into the hidden canyon.

Maggie was stunned. It was even more beautiful than she had remembered it. There was a beaver pond forming a pool near the center of the hidden canyon, a small waterfall on the back wall, and then there was the fantastic Victorian mansion sitting on the ledge dominating everything.

"Oh, my," she said, breathless, just stopping and staring. He had painted the mansion a deep blue, with white trim. The wooden shakes on the roof were coated in a way that they seemed to glisten in the early morning light. The railing along the front porch was white and shone as well. And she could see a couple places to sit on the big front porch.

She looked over at Dan who as just sitting on his horse and staring at her.

"That is fantastic!" she said. "This entire canyon is fantastic, but that home... Wow, it is completely stunning. How in the world did you build that here?"

Dan smiled, clearly pleased. "One cut, one nail at a time."

"You did all of that on your own?" she said, looking back at the house above them, seeing the massive stone fireplaces on both sides of the home, the tall, peaked roofs.

"I did," he said. "For the first few years I lived in what I now use as a shed and a shop for woodworking."

He pointed to a standard log cabin she hadn't noticed before that was to the left of the big Victorian. It hadn't been there when she had come here a hundred plus years in the future.

"I love Victorians," she said. "I love everything about Victorians. The style, the furniture, everything. I am just stunned, completely stunned."

"Then come on up to my humble abode," he said smiling.

He led the way up the trail toward where there was a stable against the rock wall behind the home. The stable had been gone as well in the future.

Maggie just kept staring at the home. Every detail seemed perfect. She would have to ask him how he managed to get those massive windows in here.

And about a hundred other questions, but right now her mind was reeling. This was the most beautiful home she had ever remembered seeing. Even the Victorian mansion that was the headquarters for the Institute in Boise didn't compare to this one.

Tombstone Dan was one amazing human being. Of that there was no doubt. Learning how to do this kind of craftsmanship would take lifetimes. He had been a cattleman.

Then the word *lifetimes* sort of hit her and she looked at the handsome man getting off his horse near the stables.

Could he be a traveler as well?

Was that even possible that Dawn and Madison and Bonnie and Duster not know all the travelers?

He came back and offered his hand to help her from her horse.

"Sorry," she said. "Just stunned at the beauty of this home."

He beamed and then had her tie up her horse next to Jenny.

"Come on in. There is so much more to show you."

And for the next hour she got a tour of the most wonderful home she could ever imagine.

Every detail was perfect.

And it shouldn't have been.

PART FIVE
The Problem of Time

THIRTY-ONE

Monumental Valley, Idaho
July 28th, 1909

DAN COULD NOT believe that they had made it to his home. Fourteen years of working toward this moment and he now felt so relieved and so happy that Maggie loved his home, he almost couldn't believe it.

He felt like a kid again.

When they were finished with the tour, he got them both glasses of cold water from his tap in his kitchen and they went out onto the front porch to sit in the morning sun as it crested the mountains to the east.

The air was perfect, the day perfect.

All the way through the tour, Maggie had just bubbled about the wonderful details he had managed to get in, many of them he hadn't had the first time he built this place.

She clearly knew a lot about Victorian homes, far more than had come up in any conversation. And she knew what it had taken for him to build this alone. And the years of work it had taken.

Now, sitting beside him on his front porch, she was silent, just staring at the beautiful colors on the mountains from the sunrise.

"Can I ask your thoughts?" he said. "Or would that be too bold?"

"I was thinking about a number of things," she said. "How fantastically beautiful this canyon is to start with."

"I was very lucky to find it," he said. And he knew he had been.

"I was thinking how lucky I was to learn about you and then come to meet you."

"I am the one who considers myself lucky there," he said.

"And I am worried about our secrets," she said.

He was surprised about that. "Do you mean the secret of yours that you have mentioned?"

"I do," she said, nodding. "And I have a hunch you have the same secret. The more I think about it, the more I am sure, in fact."

He sat back, not having a clue what she was alluding to.

"Your house is wonderful, the details are perfect. And that is what leads me to think your secret is similar to mine."

All he did was frown at that.

She turned to face him. "May I be very, very bold?"

He nodded. "I tend to always enjoy the outcome of such boldness."

She laughed and blushed a little.

Then her face got serious. "Would you consider living a lifetime with me in this home with you, and having children and raising them here?"

He was surprised and pleased, so he said what came to his mind right at that very moment. "I would live a hundred lifetimes with you in this home if that is what you wanted."

"I would want that very much," she said, smiling at him. "That has to be one of the nicest things anyone has ever said to me."

"Thank you," he said.

"So, let's get these secrets of ours out in the open if we are going to spend some lifetimes in this wonderful place together," she said. "Mr. Daniel Silver, Mr. Dan Gray, would you like to take me to see the tombstone and tell me the story of how you took the name Tombstone Dan?"

He blinked at her, doing his best to remember when he had told her about the tombstone of the old dead trapper he had found when he first came to this hidden canyon.

She touched his arm and leaned over and kissed him, then said, "You didn't tell me about it."

"Then how do you know?" he asked.

Now Available
from all your favorite booksellers
in trade paper and electronic editions.

She smiled and said, "Would you believe I am a great researcher?"

He frowned. "I know you are, but I have never written that down or told anyone."

"Then would you believe me if I said Dawn and Madison told me about it, because when we went over that cliff together in that last timeline, they buried us up by that tombstone together?"

Dan just sat there staring at the woman he had come to love, that he had spent the last fourteen years waiting to be with again.

How was what she was saying even possible?

The porch seemed to be spinning.

She held out her hand for him to shake.

"My name is Professor Maggie Lund. I jumped back here from July 1st, 2019, to meet you. Twice."

He stared into those beautiful golden eyes for a moment, then reached out and took her hand. "My name is Professor Daniel Silver. I came back from October 17th, 2020. This last time, after we died, just to meet you again."

She looked at him, shocked. "You spent fourteen years doing the same thing as you had done the previous timeline, waiting for me?"

"I did," he said, nodding.

She stood, pulled him to his feet and kissed him so hard, he could barely breathe.

And he kissed her back, the best kiss he could have ever imagined.

After a moment she looked up into his eyes and said, "Did you really mean living lifetimes with me, now that you know that is actually possible?"

"I did and I still do," Dan said, kissing her again.

Then he looked at her, suddenly realizing that she still knew something she wasn't saying.

"You have been here before, haven't you?" he asked.

She smiled. "In 2019. The day Dawn and Madison and Duster and Bonnie invited me to the cavern part of the Institute."

"And this place was still standing?" Dan asked.

"It was beautiful," Maggie said. "It had been preserved since about 1970 by, we think, one of our kids or grandkids. There was a picture on the mantle of you and me, much older, taken in 1934 with two grown kids. I didn't recognize myself at first because I didn't know about this timeline stuff at that point."

"I think I am going to love this timeline," he said, smiling at her and kissing her again.

And he did.

Every single minute of it.

THIRTY-TWO

Monumental Valley, Idaho
September 12th, 1937

MAGGIE SAT BESIDE the man she loved as he fought to catch his breath. She had helped him out to his chair on the front porch of their Victorian home in their wonderful hidden canyon so he could watch the sunrise as they had done so many thousands of times together.

Both their kids, Tom and Cindie, were here as well. Their spouses and the grandkids had been left at home in Boise. At the moment both of the kids were inside, doing the breakfast dishes.

They both knew that their father had very little time left. That's why they were here.

Maggie sat beside Dan, holding his hand, as they had done so many, many times.

"Been a fun one, hasn't it?" Dan said between slight coughing fits. His once strong voice now weak with the disease tearing him apart.

"It has been wonderful," she said. "And I will be waiting for you in the living room when you get back."

At times she couldn't imagine that the cavern and the Institute and the living room had been anything more than a dream. It had been so many years. But every time they were in Boise for any reason, they stopped by and went down into the living room to remind themselves that they had a life, many lives, after this one.

And they had also gone back to their own times a few times for short trips to get modern supplies for the hidden room behind the stables.

"I hope your wait for me won't be too long," he said.

"Long enough to make me really horny I'm sure."

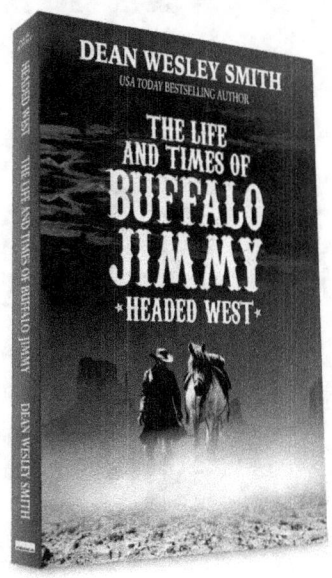
With that he laughed and then started coughing.

She got him calmed down and they sat quietly, enjoying the wonderful sunrise together.

Then Tom and Cindie helped him back to his bed and four hours later he died peacefully.

When it happened, Maggie was surprised at herself.

She took a deep breath and didn't even cry.

Now, for her, the hard part started.

She was once again without Tombstone Dan.

She had been, in this timeline, ten years younger than Dan. And she didn't want to go just pull the cords at the Institute from the timeline and leave her children wondering where their mother had disappeared to.

So she and Dan had decided she would live out her normal life. He wanted her to experience their grandkids and then tell him all about it on the other side.

He really had loved his kids and grandkids. As he said one night, that surprised him. He had never considered himself the family kind of guy.

She had said, "You called yourself Tombstone Dan. Is it any wonder?"

They had laughed for months about that, puzzling both their kids at times.

When she finally died of natural causes and returned to the cavern, she and Madison and Dawn and Duster and Bonnie would have to be very careful to make sure that none of them mentioned to Dan what they knew about his future.

And she would have to make sure she avoided seeing him.

She would return one year and three months ahead of him.

So she would have to wait through that as well, even though he was there, first as a researcher, then as a traveler.

She and Dan didn't dare take a chance of messing up the events that got them to this lifetime together.

Both her kids were strong and they went and got two of Dawn and Madison's boys from the lodge who came down to help bury Dan up by the old trapper's tombstone.

Maggie was to be buried right beside him when her time came.

So after Dawn and Madison's kids had left, and her kids were inside, she sat on the big front porch next to Dan's empty chair.

That was all she could do.

He had waited for her for fourteen years.

Now it was her turn.

THIRTY-THREE

Boise, Idaho
October 17th, 2020

DAN FOUND HIMSELF once again young and standing with his hand touching the wooden machine on the table. He had died of old age a couple times in all his trips into the past. It was never fun to go that way. But he hadn't minded this time because Maggie had been with him the entire time.

He quickly put on the gloves and unhooked the cords from the machine, then went into the cage and unhooked the cords from the crystal. Then he carefully marked on the note pad under the crystal the time and date it was used and put his name.

In the crystal above it he and Maggie had both died on the trail.

In the second crystal, they had had decades together.

Now, if everything worked out, Maggie would be waiting upstairs in the living room area.

She had been back here for over a year, at least in present day time. She might have lived a long time since their last moments together if she had gone back into the past on a lot of trips. He had lived almost a thousand years in just four months of real time.

So he just hoped she was going to be there.

And still love him as much as he loved her.

He had to trust that would be the case.

One thing he was very impressed about was how Dawn and Madison of this time period here hadn't said a word to him about anything. And Maggie had been around the Institute, he was sure,

and in his research days he hadn't even caught a glimpse of her. He would have remembered.

He left the room and sprinted for the supply room and his locker. He didn't want to see her dressed in his old man's clothes, so he quickly showered and changed into his normal jeans, dress shirt, and tennis shoes.

Would she even recognize him. He was only thirty-two years old now, the same age she was. When she had met him and fallen in love with him, he was in his forties in the past.

He made himself walk up the stairs to the large living room slowly, carefully, so he wouldn't be winded.

Then he opened the door to the living room.

No one.

He had forgotten that when he originally left twenty minutes before, two lifetimes before, no one had been in the living room. Maggie would not have dared take the chance of showing up too early to meet him and run into him before he left.

But as of this moment, they were both on the same time.

So where was she?

Then Duster's voice came out of the room behind the kitchen.

"Oh, thank god, he showered."

Laughter and then Maggie came running out and into his arms, kissing him hard and long as applause seemed to fill the cavern.

He couldn't believe how wonderful she felt in his arms.

She was crying and kissing him and not wanting to let him go and he didn't want to let her go either.

"Oh, to hell with them," Duster said after a moment. "Let's cut the cake."

At that Maggie laughed and Dan surfaced enough to look around at the other travelers standing near the kitchen counter. There had to be ten of them, including Director Parks.

All of them were smiling.

Dan looked at Maggie. "So how long did you have to wait?"

She kissed him lightly, then said, "Sixteen years, five months, three days and twenty-five minutes."

"But who's counting?" Duster said and everyone laughed.

Maggie smiled up and Dan and said, "Who knew I was from such a long-lived family?"

At that he and Maggie got lots of hugs from everyone and ate some congratulations cake.

THIRTY-FOUR

Boise, Idaho
October 17th, 2020

LATER THAT EVENING, Maggie sat beside Dan on the patio of her condo, watching the river flow slowly past. It was too late in the year and too late at night for any more rafters. The night air had a slight chill to it, even though it had been a warm fall day.

The leaves of the trees around the condo were starting to turn gold and red and the ground was already littered with them.

She couldn't believe how wonderful it felt to be beside Dan again. She had dreamed of this day since he had died and it was even better than she had dreamed.

And he was more handsome than she remembered.

She just didn't feel whole without him in her life.

Inside, over a light dinner, she had showed him pictures of their great grandkids she had stashed at the Institute in 1951. She had loved how he beamed with pride at each picture.

She had lived for fifteen more years after Dan had died, until 1952. Her kids and grandkids were wonderful to her and one of her grandchildren, a boy named Pete, married a nice girl named Nancy and they moved into the house in the hidden canyon when Maggie felt she could no longer stay there for the winter.

She hated to leave it, but the winters up there were made for the young. The last three years of her life she had lived in a home of her own out near the Morris Hill Cemetery, with help coming to cook and clean in the last two years.

She hadn't really enjoyed being elderly. But she wasn't afraid to do it again.

"So tell me," Dan said, "How did you avoid us accidently seeing each other here this last year? My condo is only about fifty paces in that direction."

He pointed along the river.

"I wasn't here," she said. "I just couldn't have been because I would have constantly been tempted to talk to you or meet you or stalk you."

"You would make a good stalker," he said, laughing.

"Look who's talking, Tombstone. You spent fourteen years stalking me, remember?"

"Worth every minute of it," he said.

"Damn, you are the sweetest man I have ever met," she said, leaning over and kissing him.

"So where did you go if you weren't here?" he asked.

"From the time they invited you here to research and then show you the caverns, I was back in Madison teaching."

"Really smart idea," he said.

It had been the only thing she could think of to do, actually, and both Dawn and Madison had thought it a great idea. And the University welcomed her back completely.

Plus her wonderful apartment on the second story of the old Victorian was still there, since the Institute had kept up the rent. It wasn't like living in her and Dan's wonderful home in Tombstone Canyon, but it helped dull the ache a little.

"And after the summer term was over in August, I finally went to visit my sister in New York. I didn't get back here until two days ago."

"You two patch things up?" Dan asked.

She had told him about her sister numbers of times. He basically had no family to talk about.

"Not really," Maggie said. "I got the obligation out of the way, though. So it is out of my head. I tried."

"Didn't sound like fun," Dan said.

"It wasn't. This is my home. You are my family."

"I feel the same way," he said, leaning over and kissing her again.

Maggie felt like she had come home, coming back to the Institute and to Boise. She had missed it.

And now Dan was sitting beside her and that felt wonderful.

Everything felt right.

They sat in silence for a little bit, enjoying the feel of the night and of being together.

Then Dan said, "We have some books to write."

She laughed. "That we do."

"You want to go back to Tombstone Canyon, build the Victorian, and write them there?"

She laughed. "Well, Mr. Tombstone Dan, are you asking me to spend another lifetime with you?"

"I certainly am," he said, smiling. "And as I said before, more than just one I hope, because I have realized that my future is nothing without you."

She just looked at the handsome man beside her, then stood and pulled him into her arms and kissed him.

"I love you more than you can know," she said. "And my future and all the pasts we travel to is nothing without you as well."

"You waited over fifteen years for me," he said, smiling. "I think I know how much you love me."

She smiled at him. "I still think you did the fourteen years of waiting for me to get back in my pants."

He smiled and said, "And mighty great pants they are. How about we go get you out of them now?"

"Wait," she said, laughing. "I'm supposed to be the one that wants to see you naked, remember?"

"I was old then," he said. "You sure you want to see this young body naked?"

She laughed and kissed him hard and then looked him right in the eyes and said, "As a favor to me."

He laughed. "Oh, I love these kinds of favors."

And as it turned out, it was a really, really fun favor.

~

Coming Next Issue in *Smith's Monthly*

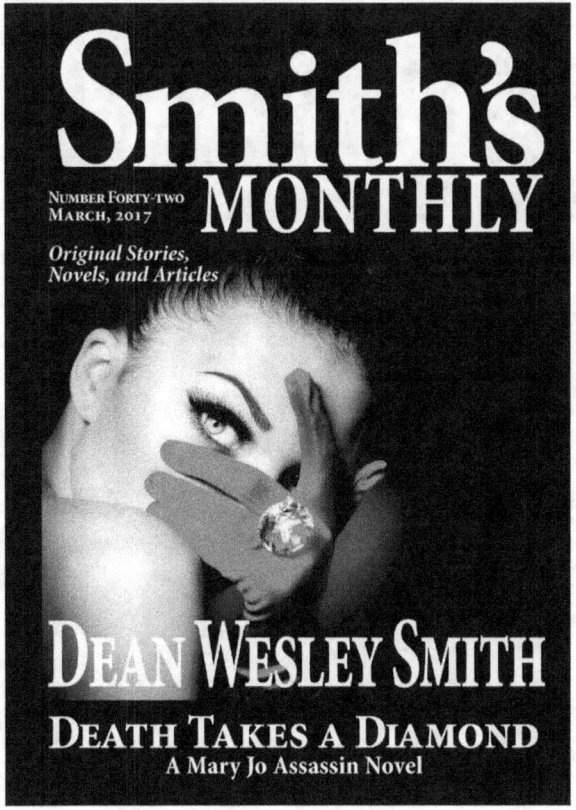

#1...October 2013

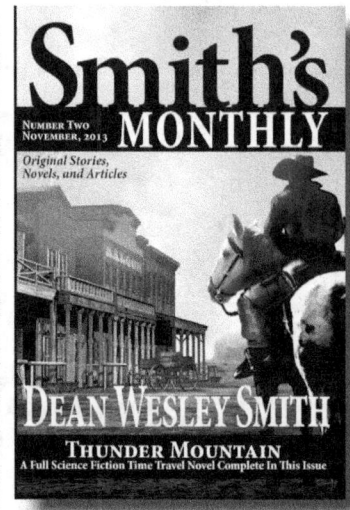

#2...November 2013

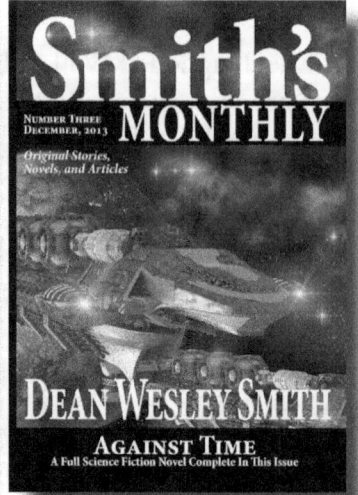

#3...December 2013

#4...January 2014

#5...February 2014

#6...March 2014

#7...April 2014

#8...May 2014

#9...June 2014

#10...July 2014

#11...August 2014

#12...September 2014

#13...October 2014

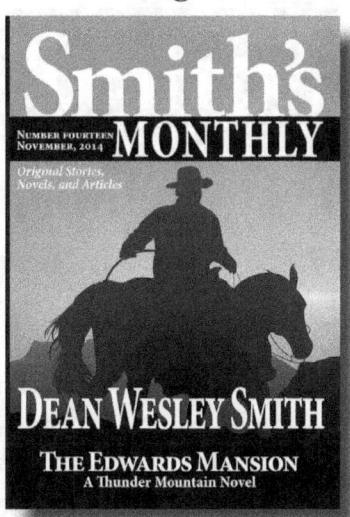

#14...November 2014

#15...December 2014

#16...January 2015

#17...February 2015

#18...March 2015

#19...April 2015   *#20...May 2015*   *#21...June 2015*

#22...July 2015   *#23...August 2015*   *#24...September 2015*

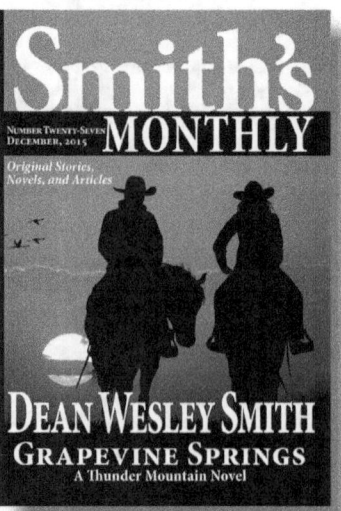

#25...October 2015   *#26...November 2015*   *#27...December 2015*

#28...January 2016

#29...February 2016

#30...March 2016

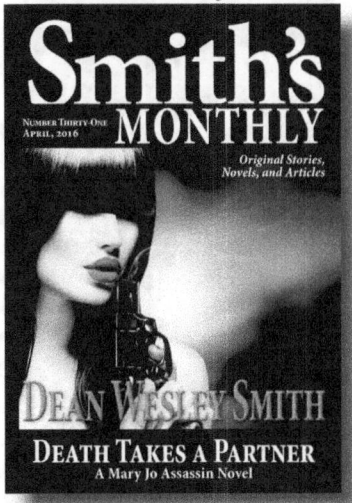

#31...April 2016

#32...May 2016

#33...June 2016

#34...July 2016

#35...August 2016

#36...September 2016

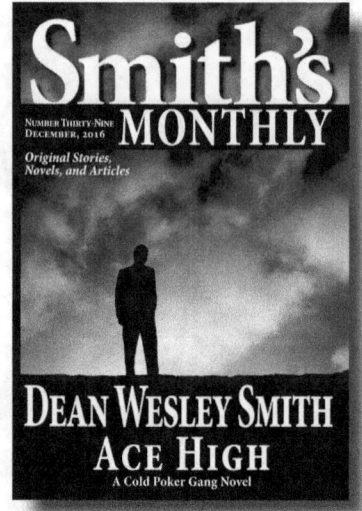

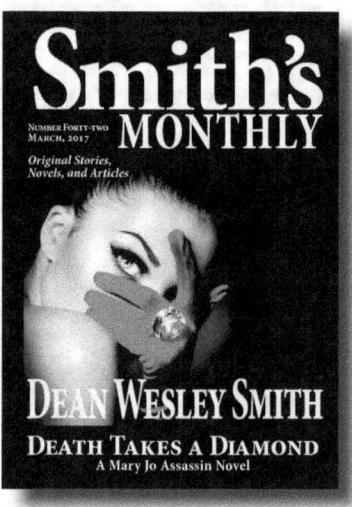

Thank You!!

I would like to thank the following wonderful people
who support my blog and my work through Patreon.
Your support is very important to me. Thanks!

Irette Y Patterson
Kathryn Rooney
Erick Lindman
Christopher Ridge
Raphael Husbands
James Gotaas
milady133
Danica Oakley
Kenny Norris
Kate MacLeod
Leah Cutter
Leigh Anderson
Robert J. McCarter
Jennette Heikes
Jamie Curierre
Albert Lemke
Marsha Kessler
Diane Darcy
Robin Brande
James Husum
Terry Mixon
Shantnu Tiwari
Chong Go
Maria Grace
Gnondpom
David Hendrickson
Fen

Sherman Cox
Miguel Angel Alonso Pulido
Marian Goldeen
Michelle Tatam
J.R. Murdock
Gunnar Gunderson
Jesse P Thurston
coraa
Martin Barkawitz
David Beers
Leslie Claire Walker
Nancy Hendrickson
F.I. Goldhaber
Michael J Lawrence
Barbara G. Tarn
Anthony St. Clair
Ann Tucker
Karl Gallagher
T. Thorn Coyle
Cristof Jones Harrison
Tasha Turner Lennhoff
Brenda Smith
Kari Wolfe
Mary Jo Rabe

And a very special thank you to
Betsey Wilcox.